To Bonnie—
aloha,
Nancy Hill

For more information regarding this novel or its authors, visit;

www.thepointoforigin.webs.com
thepointoforigin@hotmail.com

The Point of Origin

An Awakening...

Duke and Nancy Kell

Two Ton Productions
Hawai'i, USA

ISBN 978-0-578-06036-1

Two Ton Productions
Kona, Hawai'i, USA
www.twotonproductions.webs.com

First Edition

For "Cobos"

Acknowledgments

We would like to begin by thanking Oprah Winfrey, whose segment on "The Secret", laid the foundation for our understanding of the power of positive thinking; followed by J.R. Parrish, whose guidance played an integral role in our maturation. Finally, we would be amiss, if we did not thank our family, friends and students, who continue to inspire us daily.

Truth…..

❖ Oraibi is the oldest, continually inhabited settlement in North America. It is registered as a National Historic Landmark.

❖ All Hopi words are used in the context of their actual meanings.

❖ The Hopi Indians have a prophecy about the creation of the world.

❖ Hopi elders have spoken to the United Nations several times regarding their prophecy. They have attempted many more times.

❖ *The Phoenix Gazette* did in fact run a story on April, 5, 1909, about G.E. Kincaid's discovery.

Chapter One

Reaching into his tweed trousers, a tall, graying man fumbled his keys as he pulled them from his pocket. The keys suspended in the air for a brief moment before careening to the ground. The piercing sound echoed throughout the hallway, heightening his anxiety. As he reached down, he distraughtly scanned the area. Then he hastily grabbed his keys and lifted them up towards the keyhole. Before he could get his keys into the door, a hand reached out and clutched his shoulder. The Professor jumped and nearly fell down trying to get away. A handsome, blond lab assistant asked, "You OK Doc? I didn't mean to startle you."

"Brian, it's you."

"Here let me get that for you." He reached out and stuck his own key into the door then turned it. "Seriously Sir, you look like you just saw a ghost. Are you feeling OK?" The Professor didn't say anything he just nodded. It didn't seem like he was paying attention to Brian at all. He just kept looking around intently, staring at and sizing up every person within view. Brian waived his hand in front of the Professor, "You OK?" This time, he seemed to snap back into reality. "I'm fine. Why don't you take the day off? I'm only going to be here for a few minutes." Brian was astonished, this was highly unusual.

As he held the door open for the Professor, he quizzically asked, "Don't you think I should do the observations for the day? Missing a day could negate this entire round of the experiment, our research would be void." The Professor didn't answer he just walked by, preoccupied with his thoughts. Brian answered himself, "I'll take that as a yes." The Professor walked straight over to the desktop computer at his workstation in the lab and turned it on. Brian walked over to a changing area where a drawn fabric curtain served as a privacy room. The energy lab was overly cautious, and required all lab assistants and other staff working with the Professor's secret research to wear safety suits. Brian sat down behind the green curtain on a cold metal bench. He was facing a small locker with a combination dial on the front. He reached down and untied his shoes. The Professor, frantically moving files on his desktop, thought to himself, *I need to hurry.*

Suddenly a bullet ripped though the Professor's navy blue, sport jacket and shattered the screen in front of him.

***

I don't think they saw me, in fact I know they didn't see me. Why else haven't they killed me? Maybe they're still here. Maybe they haven't left. Man, I wish I could see the clock. How long has it been? The silence was like the agony of nails on a chalkboard, fear had taken grip of his neck. There is nothing more terrifying than silence, knowing that you are alone and death is waiting. *Screw it. I'm running for it.*

Out from behind a giant wet processing platform, and between two hanging dividers that separated the lab, Brian sprinted. Without hesitation he ran straight past the sprawled out body of the Professor, crashing through the lab door and into a crowded college corridor. He reached his hands up and yelled, "Call 911, he's been shot!" then collapsed onto the linoleum floor.

Chapter Two

"I told you, I came in late for my lab duties and found him lying there on the floor. When I realized he was shot, I ran out the door and yelled for help." The long and lanky detective slowly walked back and forth in front of the table. At each turn he took a long drag off the smoldering cigarette hanging from his lip. He blew the smoke out of his nose, as he grilled the young, blue eyed lab assistant from the Colorado School of Mines. "Brian, can you please explain to me, how is it that you knew he'd been shot?"

The cocky lab assistant was accustomed to talking his way through most situations, but this was different. A small bead of sweat accumulated on the top of his brow, his hands began to grow clammy and tremble. "Look, I walked in, saw a hole in his chest, then turned around and ran out."

The detective took one last drag then walked out of the door and into the next room. On the other side of the two-way mirror, there were standing two of Golden's finest police officers. Sandy, was a redheaded firecracker, she lived life fast and made no apologies. She was perched against the corner of a cold, steel interrogation table. Her partner and best friend, Ben, was leaning against the wall at the back of the dimly lit room. Ben had dark hair that was cropped short and a warm, friendly smile. "Well, he's lying to us. I can see it in his eyes." Before Captain Barba had a chance to answer, Sandy chimed in, "We can't go to the chief or the district attorney without some kind of evidence."

Captain Barba had a stomach that hung over the front of his belt and his graying hair was starting to recede. While on the job, he had never been one to play well with others. He spoke as he walked towards the door, "Cut this one loose. Put a tail on him, if he's our doer, he'll slip up, they always do."

Chapter Three

Knock, knock, knock. "Who's pounding on the door?" A beautiful blond slipped her slender legs out of the sheets, and ran her fingers though Brian's blond hair. She grabbed a t-shirt off of the floor and pulled it over her perfect naked silhouette. Then she stumbled over the clothes piled on the floor as she reached for the handle, and clumsily flung the door open to see a visibly irate brunette woman standing there.

"Where is Brian Brady?" The blond looked as if she had just been caught with her hand in the cookie jar. "Uh, well, look he never told me he had a..." The brunette rudely interrupted her, "Look Goldilocks, get out of my boyfriend's room or else."

Meanwhile, down the hall, tucked behind a corner, Ben was on the radio with the Captain. "Sir, um, we seem to have a problem."

"What kind of problem?" Ben squirmed and looked back down the hall. "Well Sir, you know the Professor's daughter?"

"Yes."

"Well, last night, Sandy and I might have let it slip that we were suspecting the lab assistant. And, well Sir, she is standing in front of, cancel that, going into Brian Brady's room right now." The voice on the other end of the walkie-talkie was full of utter contempt and disgust. "You stay put, and watch their every move."

Chapter Four

Brian was now groggily waking up from one too many margaritas at the Rio last night. His vision was just coming into focus. "Thanks a lot Brian! I thought you were different." The blond woman began putting on her pants and collecting her things as she made her way out the door. The brunette was waiting for the blond to exit the cramped but tidy dorm room before walking out of the shadows.

"Who the hell, are you?"

Chapter Five

Two men wearing dark suits came barging into the Captain's office unannounced. "I told them you were busy Sir" the secretary apologized. "Captain Barba?" the taller man asked. "Yes. What is the meaning of this?" Both men simultaneously reached into their jacket's inner pockets, revealing holsters and guns as they pulled out their identifications. The shorter of the two spoke, "Sir, we are here on behalf of Homeland Security." They flashed their credentials to the Captain. "We are here to inform you that the Gerardo case is now in our hands."

The Captain took his hand off the secured Smith & Wesson under his desk and stood up. "What? This is a local murder, why are the feds taking over? It hasn't even been twenty-four hours." The two men stepped a little closer to the desk and the taller man reached out his hand. "I'm Agent Pope, and we are not at liberty to disclose any information about the case. What we need right now, is everything you currently have." The Captain interrupted him, and brusquely let go of Agent Pope's hand. "So, two men walk in here with some nice suits and fancy Id's, and I'm supposed to just accept what you're telling me?" Agent Pope was now becoming a little agitated, he pulled out his phone and pushed a few buttons then he handed it to the Captain.

Chapter Six

The tall, dark haired woman standing steadfast in front of Brian was unable to form the words to say anything. Brian asked her again as he sat up, "Who are you and what are you doing in my room?" Suddenly, she reached out and slapped him. "Why are you lying? Did you kill my Dad?" Brian, now realizing who this woman was, moved back up against the wall, trying to distance himself from another blow. "I said why are you lying?" Brian was confused and unsure how to answer her question. "I don't even know what you're talking about."

She quickly jumped up on top of the twin bed and straddled Brian like a lion pouncing on its prey, wrapping her hands tightly around his neck. Out of instinct, Brian flipped her over and sat on top, holding her wrists so that she could not make any more connections with her clawing nails. "Are you going to kill me now?" she shrieked. Brian was shocked. "I didn't kill your Dad." She struggled to try and free herself. "Your name is Tiffany, isn't it?" Her mind was racing. *Maybe I didn't really think this through before coming here.* If this really was the killer, then she was in big trouble. "It's Tiffany, right?" Brian asked again, trying to calm her down. "Let me go!" She squealed. "Only, if you promise not to hit me again."

"OK." Brian let go, then helped her to sit up and quickly moved to the other side of the dorm room. "It's Tiffany, isn't it? Your Dad spoke of you often. Your senior thesis is the stuff of legends around here."

"Why did you lie?"

"What do you mean? I didn't lie about anything, and I didn't kill your Dad." Tiffany jumped up off of the bed and moved closer to Brian. "My Dad would never accept a lab assistant to come into his lab late, and I mean never." Brian realized that she was right. He remembered back to the first day in the lab, the Professor had explained, that if he was ever late, he would be locked out and dropped from the class. It was pretty well known by most of the physics students, that the Professor never gave empty threats. Brian and Tiffany were at a standstill, no sound, no movement, just silence and then more silence.

Chapter Seven

Ben was still standing in Bradford Hall, looking down the large hallway across to Brian's door. Suddenly he heard his radio, it made him jump and he quickly replied, "This is Lovato." The radio squawked back, "Ben, back to the station."

"But Cap..." The Captain cut him off. "The feds are here and we're no longer on the case." Ben was frustrated and perplexed. Then the Captain did something that he had never done before, confusing Ben even further. "Hey, you know what, just take the rest of the day off, and enjoy yourself." Ben lived alone and had no family to speak of. He never enjoyed being off the clock. The Captain knew that, and would often joke about the amount of overtime and unpaid hours that Ben would spend working on very mundane cases. He was quite famous for solving the case of the stolen mountain bike from the Coors' Brewery, parking lot. Something strange was happening here, this was no average case.

Chapter Eight

Knock, knock, knock. Tiffany turned to Brian, "Are you expecting anyone?"

"Not that I know of, but you obviously found me. Maybe we should just be quiet and they'll go away." Knock, knock, knock. The door was pounded on one more time, but then there was a sudden silence.

All the while, down the hall, Ben was still watching intently as two men dressed in suits knocked on Brian's door. *That must be the feds, man they work fast.* A moment later, one of the men stepped back and then did a quick front kick, causing the doorjamb to splinter in every direction and the door to slam forward onto the floor. The two men rushed into the room. "Put your hands up!" Tiffany and Brian raised their hands and stared at the pair with guns aimed on them. "Now, slowly walk over to the wall and place your hands on it." Tiffany was stunned, but managed to speak, "May I ask to see your identification?"

"No, you may not." replied one of the men. He had a head that was shaved clean and it shined under the fluorescent lighting. The two men grabbed the hands of both Tiffany and Brian, and cuffed them behind their backs, then forced them to walk out of the room and down the hall to the elevators. Every person in the residence hall was watching intently, including Officer Ben Lovato. This was something that Ben had always dreamed about, a real case, with real murder, the kind of case that can make or break a law career.

He saw no reason not to take it a far as he could, and as fate would have it the elevators were right next to where Ben was standing. He decided to take a ride down with the agents and their two suspects. When he entered the elevator with the foursome, he felt an uncomfortable silence. He decided to break the ice. "So, you got your man, huh?" The agent holding Brian had a goatee and long, dark hair that was slicked back into a low ponytail. He answered Ben, "We are not at liberty to say." Tiffany had had enough.

"We haven't been read our rights, and I haven't done anything. I demand you let me go and..." Smack. A loud thud could be heard, and Tiffany suddenly crumbled to the ground at Ben and Brian's feet. Ben was surprised by what he felt had been unprovoked violence. It took everything he had not to open his mouth. "Sorry about that Sir, but we can't have terrorists running around here, now can we?" Brian, now terrified was unable to utter even a sound. Ben looked at the bald man, then at the one with the goatee. "I'm glad you guys can help keep my son safe. He attends this school and I feel better knowing you're here." A bell rang and the door opened on the first floor, the bald agent picked up Tiffany and threw her over his shoulder. They all walked out of the elevator.

Ben went in the opposite direction to try and throw off any further suspicion. He then doubled back, and exited the glass double doors of the red brick dormitory just in time to notice something that seemed out of place. Across the open grass commons, the two agents were putting the suspects into a 1966, Ford Fairlane, with a blue body and a white rag top. He had never seen federal agents in a classic car before, and certainly not one in mint condition. He also found it strange, that when they left the picturesque college campus behind, they were heading west. Ben's unmarked Chevy Caprice, patrol car made following them pretty easy. *Why are they headed west? There's nothing but mountains and some old mining towns up this road. Since when do the feds use old mining towns to set up shop?* After fifteen minutes of tailing the agents, he saw the Fairlane put on its blinker and head up Saint Mary's Glacier Road.

Chapter Nine

Saint Mary's Glacier is one of the last remaining glaciers in the Colorado Rockies. Her pristine waters drip into a lake at the base of the magnificent glacier. During the winter months, this area is covered with a thick, white blanket. However, the warmth of the summer sun melts away all of the snow except for the glacier itself. The effect is always crystal clear, but cool mountain air. The deep blue lake is like a twinkling sapphire surrounded by emerald green pines.

The road to the glacier is a dead end. Ben knew this, so he waited a couple of minutes then headed up after them. *What am I doing? First thing you learn at the academy, never go in without backup.* Despite his misgivings about continuing the pursuit, Ben pulled into the dirt parking area. He knew this area like the back of his hand. He had spent a lifetime running in these hills as a young track star. However, time had changed his once athletic body into a much more round, shapely figure.

Pulling up beside the empty Fairlane, Ben started to get a very bad feeling in the pit of his stomach. He reached down to his radio and remembered that there was no service up here. At this point there was no turning back. He was here and there was nothing that could satisfy the questions he now had, nothing but the answers. Answers that he was sure he wouldn't find unless he hurried up. *Come on, one leg after the other. Just like old times, minus fifty pounds or so.* As he came around the corner, he found himself halting in disbelief.

Chapter Ten

The Captain walked out of the room. He went over to the coffee machine and started to pour himself a cup of the thick, dark sludge. In the background, the feds seemed to be making themselves at home in the station's conference room. The Captain yelled into the room. "If you guys want some coffee, you're more than welcome to help yourselves." Agent Pope leaned his head out of the door. "Looks like we'll be here a while, so I'm sure we'll take you up on that." He was unsure what Agent Pope was referring to when he said, a while, he could only hope that meant hours and not days.

The Captain yelled over to Sandy. "Hey Sandy, could you show me where the sugar's at?" Sandy turned, and looked at her boss as if she might kill him on the spot. *How dare he give me any sexist remarks?* She stood up and walked over to the coffeemaker. The Captain sensed that his comment did in fact hit the cord he had wanted. He made a motion with his hand indicating for her to follow him. Then he turned and walked into the small, dark supply closet just behind the refrigerator. She reluctantly followed.

Chapter Eleven

Ducking behind a large Manzanita bush, he was stunned to see two naked bodies, posing for what looked to be pornographic photographs. One of the men was taking pictures, while the other was pointing a gun, at none other than Brian and Tiffany.

"These should be enough to link you two together and give the appearance of motive." Brian screamed back at the man. "Motive, why would this give us motive? Just let us put our clothes on and let me call my lawyer!"

"You don't get it kid, we're not cops." The man with the camera gleamed. This was enough for Ben. He stepped out from behind the bush. "Drop your weapons and put your hands where I can see them." The bald man with the gun slowly dropped his weapon to the ground and began to raise his hands. The camera man instantly reached out with a gun and fired. Ben dove to the ground and returned three shots, dropping the camera man dead. The bald man, dove off of the embankment and went rolling down the side of the mountain. Tiffany and Ben were lying motionless on the frozen dirt, naked and scared to death. Ben asked them, "Are you guys OK?" Tiffany and Brian both looked at each other and then answered, "I think so."

As Ben followed Brian and Tiffany down the path, he reminded them, "Now, this sill doesn't mean that you two are out of the woods yet. The feds are at the station and I was unable to radio for any backup. So, you should probably prepare yourselves for a pretty tough interrogation."

"We haven't done anything wrong." Brian said. "Sometimes that's the last thing that matters in our system." Tiffany spoke up, "I went to Brian's dorm room to confront him, because I thought..." Ben stopped her, "I want to remind you that I am a police officer and anything you say can..." Tiffany jumped back in, "Look, I have nothing to hide, why..." Ben interrupted her again, "I work in a small town and don't have a lot of experience in these situations, but I do know that what just happened to you is one of the strangest things I've ever seen."

Suddenly, the bald man that had fallen down the mountain, jumped out in front of the threesome walking down the trail. He was brandishing a firearm, visibly wounded and stumbling towards Brian, who was in the lead. Ben, who had never used his gun before today, had already killed one person. He reacted instantly yelling out, "Get down!" Brian and Tiffany dove off of the trail and into the nearby bushes. Ben drew his weapon.

Two shots were fired simultaneously, one by the bald assailant and the other by Ben. The bullet that left Ben's gun barely missed the assailant's shoulder. The other bullet came from the assailant's gun and hit Ben, who fell over backwards. Brian, who was watching in amazement, sprang to his feet and ran full speed at the bald man. He dropped his shoulder and tackled him into the bushes like he was playing in a football game. They tumbled down the hill. When he got his bearings straight, he was lying next to the gun that the man had dropped in the collision. Brian quickly picked it up and pointed it at the man who was lying unconscious on the ground and bleeding. Tiffany yelled down, "Brian, are you OK?"

"Yeah, I'm fine. I have the gun. Is Officer Lovato OK?"

"He's been shot, but he's alive." Brian began navigating the rocks as he climbed back up the hill to Tiffany and Ben. When he finally got to the top, Tiffany was bent down over Officer Lovato speaking softly and trying to console him. She turned to Brian, "I don't know if he's going to make it."

"Well, let's pick him up and get him off the trail." Surprising them both, Ben spoke with clarity. "I think it hit my shoulder. I'm going to be OK, help me up." Brian and Tiffany both helped him up. He could barely stand and seemed to be going in and out of consciousness. They stumbled past a large bend in the trail about two hundred yards from where they had started. Ben lost consciousness, and his whole body went limp. This made carrying him next to impossible on the steep, declining trail. After attempting to put Ben over his shoulder, Brian tripped and nearly dropped him down the hill. Tiffany suggested, "Look, I think we would be better off if we sat him down and made it to his car where we can call for help."

"This guy just saved our lives. There's no way we can leave him here."

"You heard him, this is far from over and we still don't know if that guy back there's dead." Brian cockily held out the gun. "I have his gun, so there's no reason to be scared of him." Tiffany laughed, "Have you ever even used a gun?"

"Earlier, you accused me of being a killer. Now, you're laughing at the thought of it?"

"Well, that was then. Obviously the situation has changed, and we need to make a decision."

Chapter Twelve

The Captain spoke quietly, "Sandy, I need you to activate his personal GPS locator."

"Why? And why are we in the closet?"

"Earlier, against my better judgment, I had Ben stay on the trail of our suspect and the daughter of the victim. I lost contact with him, and the agents he was following should've been here at least half an hour ago."

"What! You sent Ben in without backup?" The Captain puffed his chest out and stood up straight. "I didn't actually send him in, I sent him home, knowing that he would follow the men that picked up the suspect." Sandy threw up her hands in disgust, "Six of one, half a dozen of the other. It's the same thing Sir."

"It is what it is. Just activate the locator and keep this on the down low, because something isn't adding up." They exited the supply closet into the empty staff lounge. Sandy walked directly towards the server room, where Officer Nakamoto, the station's computer technology guru spent most of his time. The station was quiet and clean, it almost seemed sterile. Inside, it looked more like a hospital than a police station. It was nothing like the portrayals you see on television, but Golden was a very small town with very little crime. There was no smoke, no criminals waiting to be interrogated, no prostitutes, just neat little office spaces with flowers and pictures adorning each desk. The floors shined in the natural light that filled most of the building.

Sandy opened the heavy door and walked into the server room. A maze of storage towers were filled with a conglomeration of computers, monitors, and a plethora of blinking lights. A low hum filled the air and you could almost feel the static electricity in the room. The temperature never deviated from a two degree change above or below seventy-five degrees Fahrenheit. This temperature control was to insure stability of the computing environment. In addition, there were air ducts protruding out of the top of each tower that drew hot air into an exhaust vent, this kept the equipment cool enough to operate at maximum efficiency. Officer Nakamoto spent a great deal of time bragging about the liquid cooled processors and high tech mumbo jumbo that Sandy could care less about. All she cared about was that when she needed video of a recent street sign theft, Officer Nakamoto was the man to go to.

However, right now she needed him to locate Ben, a loyal and trusted friend. "Hey Nak, you in here?" Nak, short for Nakamoto, poked his head out from behind one of the server towers. His long slender features and almond shaped eyes were hidden behind what other officers called his Bill Gates glasses. It was widely believed that Nak didn't even need glasses, but wore them simply to look like his idol.

"Yes Ma'am."

Chapter Thirteen

Ben slowly regained consciousness, and muttered something to Tiffany as she knelt down next to him. "What was that?" she asked. He whispered, "Leave me, as soon as your cell works call Officer Sandy St. Claire. Tell her to activate my personal locator." Ben slowly reached into his pocket and retrieved a business card, he handed it to Tiffany before he slipped back into unconsciousness. She took Ben's keys and looked at Brian. "Is that enough for you?" A tear ran down her flawless olive skin. She hung her head and walked right towards Brian. He barely jumped out of the way as her long brown hair blew in the wind, whipping him in the face.

Brian, who grew up with two sisters, was well aware of the unwritten rules of women. One rule is, when a woman is upset, never, never, disagree with her. She walked down the path and Brian followed. The frigid, cool air was a grim reminder of how close they had come to death just minutes earlier. Neither one of them had ever been in any kind of trouble and now their worlds' had been turned upside down. Brian thought to himself. *When I get off this mountain, this will all be over. I'll go back to my meaningless relationships and mindless entertainment. Oh, what I wouldn't do to be watching the Nuggets on TV right now, and enjoying a nice, cold Fat Tire.*

Meanwhile, Tiffany was hatching her own plans. *OK, Brian obviously didn't kill my Dad. Then who was it, and why would they possibly want to kill him? Brian said that whoever killed him took his jump drive files and fried his computer. It has to be linked to his research on energy, but that makes no sense. I've got to see his work.* When they got to Ben's car, they saw the Fairlane that they had arrived in still parked there. Brian turned to Tiffany and smiled, "Sorry."

They got into Ben's patrol car and drove out to the highway. When they came to the stop sign, Brian was taken aback by Tiffany pulling into the left hand turn lane. "Wrong way."

"No, I know exactly where I'm going."

"Where is that?" She pulled onto the back country, mountain highway then looked at Brian coyly. "Before we head in to be questioned, I think we would be better off knowing the whole story." Brian was a little more than perturbed, he took a few deep breaths before speaking. "I was planning on..." Tiffany interrupted him, "I was planning on seeing my Dad the rest of my life! But that didn't turn out and here we are." Brian was now a little embarrassed for being so insensitive, especially to someone who was arguably the most attractive woman that he had ever seen in person. He was very cautious as he proceeded, "OK, how do you propose we go about getting the answers?"

She didn't bat an eye when she replied. "My Dad was very, very organized. He always had three copies of everything that he was working on, and kept them in different places. That would insure that if there was ever any kind of accident, like a lab assistant burning down his lab, he wouldn't lose years of work. One of the storage sites was a cabin that he spent many of his weekends at."

"If they found us, don't you think that they know about this cabin?"

"It's very unlikely that they found any information about his cabin. In fact, the cabin belongs to a friend of his, who lives back east. He gets to use the guest cabin as long as he maintains the property."

Chapter Fourteen

The Captain spoke with authority, "We just received an anonymous tip that Ben has been shot and he's up on the St. Mary's Glacier trail." Just then, Nak came bursting out of the server room with map print outs waving in his hand. He ran towards the pair standing there, tripping over a small trash can and fumbling most of his papers to the ground. "Sandy, his locator, he's up on..." She interrupted him, "St. Mary's..."

"...Glacier trail." he finished the sentence then they both turned to the Captain. Captain Barba had worked on the north side of Denver for more than twenty years. He spent a lot of time working with kids, even teaching a life skills class at Manuel High School before it was shut down. He continually joked about how landing the captain's job up in Golden was like early retirement. It was so much easier than the job in the city had been that it was almost absurd to him. However, today, this job became real, and he took to it naturally, like a duck to water.

"Boys we got ourselves a situation here!" Everyone in the station, including the two agents who had taken over the investigation turned and walked towards the Captain. "We've got a man down and a lot of questions. I need every available unit called in." He turned and pointed at Sandy. "Take two units up there right now."

"There are already two units up there." Nak interjected. "I activated the automatic distress call when we got the tip. I think that officers should be there by now."

"Alright then, by the time Sandy gets up there the site will be prepped for our investigation. What's everyone standing around for? Let's go!"

Chapter Fifteen

Brian and Tiffany's stolen Chevy Caprice pulled up to an amazing two story, log cabin perched on a hill, overlooking an awe inspiring mountain valley. The valley was filled with Colorado Blue Spruce pines and Aspen trees as far as the eye could see. The front of the three story cabin was shimmering in the sun. Two enormous walls of glass came together at an angle protruding forward and then peaking up towards the sky into a point, creating a breathtaking sight. The cabin's trim work was entirely made of intricately carved granite stones instead of standard wood. Towering, lodge pole totems stood guard on either side of the impressive glass structure. "This is your Dad's cabin?"

"No. The main house, Mr. Downs owns. He lets my Dad use the guest quarters." They pulled around the back of the main house. Beyond a bend in the road, tucked behind the pines, was a modest little cabin. They pulled up to its front door and exited the car. The smell of pine permeated the air, but couldn't break the tension Brian was feeling. As they walked towards the door, Brian could feel his heart begin to race. *What am I doing? What if there's someone in there? What if...* Tiffany answered, as if she could sense his worry. "There's nothing to worry about out here. This is a ten acre property with only one way in." He was a little bit relieved. "We should just be able to get what we need and head back to town, right?" Tiffany did not answer. He repeated, "Head back to town, right?"

Tiffany ignored Brian and reached under the doormat to grab the spare key. When she came up, she said, "Shall we?" She put the key in the door and turned the handle.

Chapter Sixteen

At the bottom of the St. Mary's Glacier trail, a Flight for Life helicopter had just landed. A loud thumping sound, dirt and leaves were all swirling around in the air as the blades spun. The paramedics were loading up Officer Lovato. Sandy's patrol car pulled up quickly, the tires skidded in the dirt as she pulled the car sideways, sliding to a halt. She jumped out of the car and ran towards Ben on the stretcher. Officer Tippet grabbed her. "There's nothing you can do. He's lost a lot of blood and he's unconscious." The helicopter's door slammed shut as the thumping grew louder and it began to lift off of the ground carrying Ben away into the sky.

Sandy, and Ben had grown up down the street from one another, they had been friends since they had gone to elementary school together in north Denver. This was a devastating blow to Sandy, and Officer Tippet tried to console her by redirecting her thoughts. "The best thing, we can do right now, is pull ourselves together and figure out what went wrong here tonight." Sandy was visibly shaken, and the tears rolled down her cheeks. "You're right. We need to find the people that did this."

Changing the subject, Officer Tippet said, "Check this out. We've got some footprints over here." Sandy stopped dead in her tracks. "Where's Ben's car?" Officer

Tippet was obviously embarrassed by missing it. "I'll call it in."

Chapter Seventeen

Within minutes, a red light started blinking on the dashboard of Officer Lovato's patrol car, which Brian and Tiffany had driven to her Father's cabin. No one was in the car to see that the GPS locator had been activated. Meanwhile, inside the small cabin Tiffany and Brian were frantically combing over the somewhat unorganized research left behind by Tiffany's Father. This felt all wrong to Tiffany. *Why is it so disorganized? He must have really been in a hurry.*

Brian was frustrated, "There's nothing in this drawer." Tiffany was busy looking at files on the laptop. It had been left sitting on the old, distressed farmhouse table in the middle of the cabin. Suddenly, Tiffany sprang to her feet, "Holy crap!" Brian, startled by her outburst, nearly fell over backwards as he stumbled over the files that were piled on the hardwood floor. "What did you find?"

"We gotta go."

"What, why?" Tiffany pulled the power adapter from the outlet in the wood paneled wall, turned off the laptop and closed it. She picked it up and headed out the door. Although Brian was apprehensive, he followed along like a little puppy dog. They immediately headed for the car and got in. When they sat down, they noticed the blinking, red light on the dashboard of Officer Lovato's unmarked patrol car. Brian had been a police scout in high school and had done many ride-alongs. He knew exactly what the light meant. "You see this blinking light. This means they have activated the GPS locator. In other words, the police will probably be here any minute."

"Get out of the car." She turned the car off and opened the driver's door. "I said let's go." Brian didn't move a muscle he looked straight ahead as if he was in a trance. "I'm not going. I'm waiting for the police." Tiffany began pleading with a new sense of urgency. "Look, I can't explain, but I think my Dad found proof of extraterrestrial life, and I think the government might have killed him. The police may be involved too."

"What? Are you smoking something?"

"No, and if you stay here, you may be in danger." She turned and walked away.

Brian sat in the car for thirty seconds, waiting in silence. *How is it I've got myself into this, and why am I still sitting here?* He sprang out of the passenger seat, and hurried after Tiffany in the direction of the main house. He suddenly heard a loud roar, and saw an old, blue, CJ7 Jeep come flying out from behind the house. The tires continued spinning as the back end fishtailed and came to a stop inches from Brian's feet. "You coming?" Tiffany asked as she shifted gears. Brian didn't hesitate he grabbed a hold of the roll bar and jumped into the Jeep. "Let's go." She pushed on the gas pedal and pulled the emergency brake at the same time, turning around the Jeep in the right direction and throwing dirt everywhere. She then pushed down on the gas and they flew around the bend and out of the trees.

Chapter Eighteen

The pilot of the Bell, Flight for Life helicopter lowered it onto the roof of St. Anthony's Hospital. A doctor and three nurses all dressed in blue came running out to meet the patient. The doors swung open and the paramedics inside flew out with Officer Lovato on a stretcher, tubes were already coming out of his body in every direction. "He's lost a lot of blood. We have a through and through GSW to the left side, upper thoracic area."

One of the nurses answered from behind her mask. "We'll take it from here." They wheeled him straight to the operating room. The Captain, who had just arrived, was standing at the door as Ben was wheeled by. He put his hand out, but Ben had no response. He watched as the medical team pushed Ben's stretcher into the operating room. The Captain took a deep breath, raised his hands and ran his fingers through his graying hair, while shaking his head in frustration.

Chapter Nineteen

All the while, Sandy, along with two police units from Golden, Colorado, turned onto a dirt road way up in the mountains. They were heading up to the signal that Officer Lovato's car was putting off. Sandy noticed a blue Jeep exiting the road at the same time. She was so focused, that she thought nothing of it as they raced past it. On the way up the road she couldn't help but think of Ben fighting for his life back in the hospital. *I'll find the people responsible, if it's the last thing I do.*

A tear welled up in her eye. She quickly wiped it away and began to cough. This had been a common technique Sandy had used throughout her entire life, her way of hiding emotions. *In a man's world, there is no place for emotion.* Her Father used to tell her this often when she was growing up. She found that becoming a peace officer made it even more important. On the force, any sign of weakness was frowned upon. "Sandy, are you there?" A young police officer stood at the car window, knocking. Sandy came out of her daydream and back to reality. She opened the door and walked over to the empty, unmarked police car parked in front of the quaint little cabin with gingerbread trim work and green shutters.

Chapter Twenty

Tiffany and Brian were traveling west on Interstate Seventy. The Jeep had no top, and although it was summer the temperature was anything but warm. Brian yelled over the blowing wind and the rumbling exhaust noise coming from beneath his feet. "We only have a few more hours of daylight then it's really going to get cold. Maybe we should find a place to stay in Dillon." Tiffany reached back and grabbed an old, roughly woven Mexican blanket from the floor board, then handed it to Brian. "You'd better bundle up. It's going to be a couple of hours." Brian, not one to make waves, wrapped the blanket around his self and didn't bring it up again. It was difficult for him to get comfortable his tall, athletic frame didn't fit easily into the Jeep. However, after ten minutes or so, he fell asleep.

A few hours later, he awoke to find Tiffany's big, brown eyes gazing into his. For a brief moment, he thought an angel was waking him up from a bad dream, but no. Instead, it was this mysterious woman who had brought him into a dangerous game. "Brian, wake up. I got us a room." He sat up straight and looked around trying to orient himself. They were parked on a steep road in an unfamiliar mountain town. "I got us a room, let's go." It was nighttime and the temperature had dropped to a chilly, forty-five degrees. When Brian stepped out of the Jeep, he could smell a faint sulfur mist in the air. "Where are we staying?"

"Right down the street at the Hotel Colorado." He immediately knew where they were and was surprised they had driven that far. "How long have I been asleep, and why are we parking way up here and not in their parking lot?"

"The lot is full, plus who knows how long it will take them to figure out what we're driving." They talked and walked at the same time, as they went down the hill towards the side entrance of the hotel. One of the oldest hotels in the Midwest, the Hotel Colorado was a built as a replica of the 16th century Villa de Medici. However, all of the rooms are decorated in the Victorian era style. The hotel is best known for the healing powers of the nearby hot springs. Many rich and famous people frequented the Glenwood Springs area throughout history. Teddy Roosevelt often stayed at the mountain hotel during his lifetime. His love for the sulfur hot springs that fed the pools across the street was well documented. The hotel was also credited with being the place where the "Teddy Bear" was created. It was rumored, that a house maid had sewn the bear for the avid hunter on one of his trips. "Why here? This is a pretty popular hotel."

"In his digital journal that I got at the cabin, my Dad said that he left a clue at his favorite hotel. As soon as we get to the room, I'll explain everything." They turned to walk up the stairs and Brian realized that there was an elderly couple listening to everything they had said. *No wonder she shut me up. I'd better be more aware.* They walked into the hotel and straight to the huge, carved staircase at its center. "Why don't we take the elevator?"

She continued to walk up the stairs as she answered. "My Dad always said Teddy never used the elevator. So, we'll never use the elevator."

They walked up the cascading staircase. The dark, brown woodwork was warm and inviting. The creaking sounds coming from the stairs themselves on the other hand, seemed eerily reminiscent of an Alfred Hitchcock movie. They walked up, past the first two stories then exited the staircase through a set of swinging double doors, as they walked down a narrow, wallpapered hallway. They came to the second from the last door on the right. Tiffany reached out and unlocked the door.

Chapter Twenty-One

The Captain walked into the station and was promptly met by two federal agents. "We need a briefing on what you know." the taller agent said. The Captain, not in the mood for small talk, snapped back, "Look, one of my guys is down, and you're up here in my face?" The shorter agent was clearly the smarter of the two. He quickly diffused the situation. "We are very concerned about you and your fellow officers. We just want to be able to offer the full power of the federal government to help with your investigation." The tall one looked completely shocked by what his partner had just said. He tugged at his partner's arm and pulled him over to the other side of the room. "What the hell are you doing?"

"Look young fella..." he cleared his throat and raised his voice, "...you may not understand this, but when an officer is shot, we need all the help we can get." As he said this, he winked at the taller agent, then turned and walked back over to the Captain. "Sorry about my partner Captain, he's a youngster and has never served any real time on the street." This impressed the Captain and softened him up. "Come with me." The two agents followed him through the station and into his office. He offered them seats in front of his neatly arranged desk, they all sat down, and he began explaining. "Here is what we know. My guy was watching our suspect's room, when the victim's daughter showed up and entered. A few minutes later, I called him and pulled him off the case. Apparently, he stayed and saw two agents take our suspect and the daughter into custody. Next thing we know, an anonymous caller phones in, indicating that Officer Lovato had been shot. We found him, and are hopeful that he will pull through. Right now, the only lead we have is his abandoned car at a cabin that was apparently used by the Professor." The short one questioned, "How can you be sure they were feds?"

"Really, I can't. And more and more, I'm thinking that something isn't adding up here." The tall man interrogated further, "What about the cabin, any clues?"

"Sandy hasn't called anything in yet."

Chapter Twenty-Two

Sitting on the small, floral Victorian settee, Brian leaned forward. "OK, I want some answers. I think I deserve to know what I'm getting into."

"In my Dad's digital journal, he left some clues for me."

"Clues? Why the hell would he need..." Tiffany snapped back interrupting, "If you would let me finish, I think you will be quite interested in what the implications are."

"How do you know what the hell I would be interested in?"

"You're right. There's a Grey Hound leaving for Denver in the morning. I suggest that you..." Brian interrupted her, "OK, I'm sorry. I just want to know what's in store for us." He smiled, then got up and squatted down next to Tiffany. He put his hand on her knee, and said softly, "I need to know." Something about his big blue eyes and dimples made it impossible for her to resist.

Tiffany took out her Father's laptop and Brian sat down next to her as she read the last entry;

"I've made a breakthrough that will change the world, but this discovery I fear is one of immense danger. After leaving the site, I couldn't get it out of my head that

something was wrong. I had called my friend earlier and sent a photo of the artifact that White Feather and I had found. I expected to hear back from him in a couple of days, but he called back within minutes. It was the most excited he had ever been. He spoke of tales of Atlantis and ties to the Mayan myths. He also spoke of how there was some kind of 2012 prophecy. I cut him off, and asked him what this meant. He said that what I had was a picture that completed a secret ancient text. The text foretells the future and reveals our true past. What do you mean true past, I asked? As he spoke I couldn't believe my ears. How could this be I asked myself? When I hung up the phone, I headed back to the site. There was no way I could leave something that important in an unguarded cave. When I got to the cave, I discovered that I was too late, and the artifact was already gone. I knew White Feather must have come back for it. I drove to White Feather's trailer and parked at the general store across the street. I walked slowly and crossed over into his property. There was a car that I didn't recognize parked in front of the door. In the back seat, I noticed the artifact. The biggest discovery in history was in the back seat of an old Buick, with the seat belt buckled around it. However, my attention was grabbed away by a scuffle in the trailer. I tip toed over to the window, where I saw two men in suits holding pistols at White Feather. The bigger one spoke, "This is your last chance, who else knows about the artifact?" White Feather didn't say a word. He just laughed and spit blood onto the floor. The man raised his hand and hit White Feather with the butt of the gun, sending him and the chair that he was sitting on flying to the ground. I turned and headed straight to the back door of the car, hoping that it was open. By sheer fate, the door was unlocked. I quickly opened the door and unbuckled the artifact. I picked it up and walked back to my car. The weight of it was very deceptive. Although it looked to be solid stone, this stone cube was quite light. It felt like I was carrying a box of feathers. Just as I stepped into the parking lot of the store, I heard three gun shots. For the first time, I realized that this thing that I was holding must be real. What I was carrying was in fact what my friend had claimed it to be. I got in my car and got out of there before ever being seen. I knew that they would discover I was with White Feather when we had found the artifact, and it wouldn't be long before they found me. So I hid the cube, and left clues that only you would know. If you are reading this, the only way to find proof of extraterrestrial life and get the keys to our future, is to follow the trail;

Clue #1
I stay with a woman
who always stayed afloat.

Brian did not quite know what to make of what he had just heard. "Why would a world famous physicist, be interested in ancient prophecies?"

"The verbiage is very important. He said our true past. In his *Dialogues with Timaeus and Critias*, Plato spoke of the power sources of Atlantis. He may have stumbled upon that source. Maybe that's why they were after him. I'm not sure about the extraterrestrial reference, they may be connected. The point is they must be the ones who are after us."

"Who are they?"

Chapter Twenty-Three

Officer Lovato was lying on a surgical table, with a bright light, illuminating his upper body. From out of the darkness came several pair of arms covered in hospital blues. Two of the hands were pumping a ventilator, up and down. His chest was rising and descending slowly, at the same pace as the pump. The two limbs closest to the wound moved in a symphony of movements, their mirror image hung above Ben's body. The suction of gargling blood completed the orchestra, by accompanying the masterful precision cuts. Tubes protruded into the wound in the top, left chest area. A voice came from the arms conducting the orchestra, it asked for, "Scalpel, retractor and suction." The same steady, calm, never wavering voice spoke, "Here's the artery it hit, forceps." The other arms never answered, but they reacted like magic. Appearing and disappearing like a well oiled machine. Each time, handing the cardiothoracic surgeon whatever he asked for, always at a frantic pace. Within another two minutes, the doctor clapped his hands, and walked away into the darkness. "OK, boys, stitch him up."

A new set of hands, far less graceful but still capable of doing a simple interrupted stitch, entered the scene. From the wings, yet another voice asked, "Should we pull off the bag and go straight to O_2?" The set of hands now doing the sutures answered in an agitated voice, "Are you askin', or are you tellin', cause you'll never get out of your internship if you can't make a decision on your own."

Chapter Twenty-Four

"Right now, I'm not sure who they are. All I know, is someone wants the information that got my Dad killed." She put her head down to hide the tears that she just couldn't hold back. In an instant, Brian saw that maybe, just maybe, she was human. Up until this point she had seemed so cold and lifeless. He stood up, walked over to the door and turned back around. "I lost my Dad to cancer a few years back. Sometimes, it's best to just let it out. I'm going to get us some food. Do you have any preferences? I saw a Subway down the street." Tiffany said nothing at first then lifted her head, "No veggies please." Brian exited the room.

He walked slowly down the hallway admiring the pictures of all the famous patrons from the hotel's past. When he was a kid, his family had gotten to stay here once. His Father had told him that there were ghosts in the basement, and the pictures that lined the hallways all had an eerie stare for whoever was walking by. He felt a chill go down his spine as he reached out and pushed the down button on the elevator. When he looked up, a portrait of Teddy Roosevelt was staring him in the eyes. The doors opened and he entered the elevator. The interior looked like something out of an old Western movie. He couldn't help but wonder about who had been in this elevator in the past.

Chapter Twenty-Five

The tall, dark and handsome surgeon walked out of the operating room. He headed straight to the washbasin and delicately pulled off his surgical gloves, then went to work on washing his arms and hands. He felt a tap on his shoulder, and turned around to find a beautiful brunette standing there. "How is he? Is he going to make it?" The doctor, not accustomed to people in the operating room, grabbed her by the elbow and walked her outside of the careening double doors. He turned to her. "Are you the next of kin, or the spouse?"

She looked a little upset, taken aback really. Rarely did anyone talk to her so rudely. "Actually, I am a reporter for Denver 9 News. People have a right to know if there's a killer out there running loose." The doctor knew exactly who Ms. Levine was. She was infamous in the Rocky Mountain area. She had done a variety of stories that exploited the misfortunes of others. "I know who you are, and I have no comment." Right at the same moment, Sandy walked in the door and right past Lily Levine. "Any comment?" Lily stuck out the microphone, but received the hand and the back of the door, as Sandy and the doctor passed.

Chapter Twenty-Six

Brian walked into the room carrying two sub sandwiches. He placed them on the round, wooden coffee table in front of the television then walked into the bedroom where he found Tiffany asleep on the bed. He put the subs into the refrigerator and placed an extra blanket over Tiffany. He turned off the lights, walked over to the settee, kicked off his shoes and laid down. It didn't fit his long frame, but it was still better than the Jeep had been. Tiffany, wasn't really sleeping, she just didn't feel like talking. She was pleasantly surprised by Brian's thoughtfulness.

Tiffany had not been known to pick the best men to date. She had a thing for football players, and many of her exes were borderline psychopaths. Her Father was always trying to hook her up with his lab assistants. Somehow, they lacked the bad boy image that she so craved. She would bring home her new boyfriends, and Dr. Gerardo would turn a blind eye to the mental abuse that they inflicted upon his daughter. One of them had the nerve to tell him, "Women should be at home barefoot and pregnant." Her Father, the consummate human relations advocate, never batted an eye. He would often agree, and just try to get them to hang themselves with their own ignorant statements. Then, he would make comments to

Tiffany when they were alone, usually questioning the IQ and or the manhood of the current boy. This never seemed to stop Tiffany from making the same mistake over and over again. In many ways, she subconsciously wanted to repeatedly make the same decision, in order to prove to her Father that he was wrong.

Chapter Twenty-Seven

Brian was abruptly awakened by the slamming of a door. Tiffany walked into the hotel room. "They just left, we need to hurry." Brian was not privy to the plan and was still half asleep. "What is it we need to do?" He was sorry for asking, but at this point there was no turning back. Tiffany grinned and walked over to the window. "All you have to do is make sure that if anyone goes into the room next door, that you text me."

"Why? What are you going to do?"

"The suite next door is the 'Unsinkable Molly Brown Suite'. Remember the clue from my Dad's journal earlier, about the woman who never sinks? This is what he was talking about, and if I'm right, he's hidden something in the suite that will lead us to the artifact that he talked about."

"OK. But how are you going to get in the room?" The hotel had security cameras and up to date card locks on all of the doors. Tiffany lifted herself up, squatted down on the windowsill and smiled. "I think this way is the best way." Without any hesitation she turned and swung herself out of the window. Brian, in a brief moment of terror, shouted, "Don't!" He ran straight over to the window as he was blinded by the early morning sunlight.

When he reached it, he looked out, terrified that she may have fallen to the ground below. Instead, there she was, scaling the ledge, smiling and laughing. "Brian, enough already, I'll be fine. Grab the cell and text me if you see anyone going towards the door." Brian turned, grabbed the cell phone, and exited the room.

Seen from the back of the Hotel Colorado, the vision of a young woman scaling the ledge between two windows would usually cause quite a stir in the small mountain town of Glenwood Springs. But at nine o'clock in the morning on a Sunday, it's very rare to see anyone walking around. Most of the town's people are attending one of the many churches scattered throughout the area. This played right into Tiffany's hand, and she knew it. She knew this was her opportunity. So she slowly, moved across the ornate concrete ledge, carefully grabbing onto anything that would keep her from the three story fall into the back parking lot. She showed no sign of stress, no sweat, no heavy breathing, in fact this was the first time in a long time she felt good.

A newfound clarity had taken over her thoughts. She had become a hunter, a hunter for truth. This was something that her Father had tried to explain to her, but she didn't really understand what he was talking about. He had tried many different ways, but she now realized that it was not something you could understand until it happened to you. Athletes commonly experience this feeling, some call it the zone, or the runner's high. It is the moment when time slows, and everything seems within your grasp, the impossible becomes the possible. She had felt this from the second she had read her Father's words in the digital journal. She knew this was what he wanted, his dying wish, to leave her with one last present.

As she reached the window, she felt around and removed the screen. The entire scene was like poetry in motion. Never a hesitation, she was allowing the energy to flow. She refrained from thought, the essence of doubt. She swung herself around the old sash window and into the room.

She had been in this room at least ten other times throughout her life. It was one of her Father's favorite historical places. He often used Molly Brown as a model for his own daughters, who because of a rare form of cancer, called Leiomyosarcoma, lost their mother before they could ever get to know her. Now here she was, standing in a room that only day's prior, her Father had been in. *What did he leave here? Where did he leave it? How can I find the answer?*

On the outside of the room in the hallway, stood Brian filled with worry and questions. He was pacing back and forth, talking to the voice in his head. *What the hell am I doing? Why am I listening to this girl? I don't even know her. What's taking her so long?* Suddenly, on the other end of the hall, he heard the door to the elevator opening. He turned and started walking towards the family that had just exited the elevator. His heart started to beat faster. He reached into his pocket and grabbed the cell phone. *This may be them, I should call.* He opened the phone, his thumbs moved quickly over the screen. *"Someone's coming."* She quickly thumbed in a reply text, *"Stall them."* He turned to walk towards the family, but realized it was a false alarm. They stopped at another door and went in. He texted back, *"All clear."*

Still standing in the same spot in the room, Tiffany was thinking, trying to put herself in her Father's shoes. *If I was my Dad, and I was leaving a clue for me, where would I put it?* She stood there surveying the room, trying to decide where to look. Without moving, she looked with her eyes at different pieces of art and furniture, trying to decide where he would have put it. There was a sitting room, a bedroom and a bathroom. All of them were covered in textured wallpaper. Heavy draperies, upholstered furniture in floral, brocade prints and dark, carved furniture was everywhere. Not unlike a criminal, she did not want to touch anything in the room. Everything could be considered priceless pieces of art. Her Father used to tell her stories about the artwork every time they stayed there.

He was particularly interested in the highboy dresser located near the foot of the bed. He would explain how it had taken many hours of intricate design work to make. She would often roll her eyes, but usually stayed long enough to watch him show her the secret compartment that was common in furniture made during the Queen Anne period. *It has to be in the compartment right here.* She walked over to the tall dresser and opened the top center drawer. She reached in and released a wooden spring clip that opened a hidden drawer in the cornice molding directly above. She pulled it open and thick dust was covering the bottom, indicating that no one had been there for a long time. Tiffany stood on her tippy toes and looked into the empty compartment. Nothing was there.

She closed the drawer and returned to the same spot that she had stood in before. *OK, where could he have put it? And what is it, I'm looking for? Dad, come on, send me a sign. What is it? Where is it?* Her phone vibrated in her pocket indicating a phone call. Brian was standing in the hall, talking to a newlywed couple. He spoke into his phone, "Yes. Boss, I'm standing here with a couple from the Molly Brown Suite. I was explaining to them that they were chosen for a free dinner, but they need to come back down to the lobby to get their gift certificate before you leave in ten minutes." Tiffany, not quite understanding what was going on, figured this must be his attempt at stalling. "OK. Send 'em down."

"OK. No problem, but they insist on putting their bags away and then coming down." He hung up the phone, and Tiffany was flabbergasted. She wasn't sure what she should do. She went to the window and a bus was unloading right below her. She had no intention of heading back out that way. Suddenly, she heard the door knob click as the pins fell and the cylinder turned. She hastily closed the drawers and dove behind the miniature wingback chair in the back of the room, but didn't fit, so she speedily crawled over and slipped underneath the bed.

Right then, two sets of feet walked into the room. She could see one of them was a man's and the other belonged to a woman. They walked to the foot of the bed, put down their luggage, and stood there facing each other. The man's voice spoke first, "This is our honeymoon, we need to just order room service and stay in all weekend." Tiffany felt a lump in her throat. She couldn't imagine having to stay there for the whole weekend. Luckily, the female in the equation was less interested in staying in, and liked the idea of a free, five star meal. "Look honey, we have the rest of our lives for some of this..." a long pause, "...and some of that." There was another painfully long pause. Then, the male turned, and like any predictable male, walked to the door, "After you my lady."

They both walked out of the door. Tiffany knew she didn't have much time before they would return, and this time they wouldn't be nearly as happy. She rolled out from underneath the bed, and looked right at the painting hanging over the dresser. It was a depiction of the Titanic sinking into the Atlantic Ocean. She suddenly remembered her Father telling her that many of the people, who survived the ship that day, had done it by floating on a piece of furniture. She never believed the story, her Father would turn the coffee table over, and stand in it acting like it was a boat. He would call Tiffany over and say, "Hop aboard."

She ran into the sitting room, lied down on her back and slid her slender body under the solid, wood coffee table that resembled an upside down canoe. When she looked up, she saw a piece of duct tape with something underneath it. She reached up and tore it off. Underneath the tape was a small envelope, it had her name and address neatly printed on it. She quickly ripped open the envelope as she briskly walked over to the door and exited the room.

Brian was standing at the top of the stairs with their belongings and their sub sandwiches. "Did you find what you were looking for?"

"Yes. Come on let's go." She walked him to the end of the hallway where an emergency staircase led the way out. They entered through the fire door and walked down the stairs as Tiffany read the papers she had taken out of the envelope. "Well, what does it say? Can we call the police?" She kept walking, shoved the papers into her pocket and said nothing. They exited the hotel and walked towards the Jeep.

Chapter Twenty-Eight

The confident and stately surgeon walked back through the double doors and straight up to Sandy. She was standing in front of a glass window that looked out at the majestic Rocky Mountains. He put his hand on her shoulder. "Sandy, he's going to be fine." She turned, "How long, until he's back on his feet?"

"Well, the injury wasn't that bad. It was a nick to an artery that made him lose so much blood and put him in danger. A day or two of rest and he should be able to go home." A tear came to her eye and stopped her from saying anything back to the doctor, whom she knew very well. He had never seen any emotion from this woman, and he had known her since they had gone to middle school together. Along with Ben, they had been like the three musketeers.

He hugged her. "It's OK. Sandy, he's fine." Apparently, she had not expected this to affect her so much. So, she made up an excuse. "Oh. Uh." she pushed him away. "He hasn't, I mean, I'm not, I just have dust in my eyes." She turned and walked away. When she exited the double doors, Ms. Lily Levine was standing there. She was a beautiful and manipulative news reporter, who was famous for ruining people's lives using the media as her weapon.

Something came over Sandy, and before Ms. Levine could get a question out, Sandy punched her right in the nose, knocking her to the ground. She then jumped on top, and continued to hit her as many times as she could. Her arms were flailing through the air like she was an octopus. The entire time the camera was rolling, and Sandy was digging a deep hole for herself. Finally, two orderlies and a couple of nurses were able to pry her off of Lily. They helped them both up and then stood between the two creating a human wall to shield from any further cat fighting.

Right then, the Captain came walking down the hallway and saw the two women bent over with their hands on their knees and panting like tired dogs. They both looked like they had just gone through a war. "What's going on here?" Lily Levine looked up and shoved a microphone in his face. "Your officer has just assaulted me. Do you have any comments for tonight's news?" His face turned a color of red that a human face should never be, it glowed brighter than the burning sun.

He had dealt with reporters like her when he worked in Denver. One of them in particular, was at least partly to blame for the bad reputation he had gained as a hard ass. Now, that reporter's protégé was standing here shoving a microphone in his face. He wanted no part of this. "I have no comment and neither does Officer St. Claire." He grabbed Sandy by the arm and pulled her towards the double doors. The entire hospital could hear him yelling. "What are you doing here? Now, I'm going to have to suspend you!" Sandy said nothing and the Captain cooled down a little. "I know this is your partner, but you're supposed to be looking for our suspect and the woman. Why are you here?" She looked at the Captain and started to cry. "I think the best thing right now, is for you to go home and get your head straight."

"Captain, look I came here to see if I could talk to Ben. Cause honestly, I have no leads on where they're headed, and frankly nothing here is adding up." The Captain dropped his chin and looked at Sandy over the top of his glasses. "Did you hit that woman?" She couldn't lie. "Cap, I don't know what came over me, I just …"

"Look, I have to do something here. You just hit 'Prime Time Levine' she can make or break your career." Right then a nurse came out of Ben's room. "He's awake, you can see him now."

Chapter Twenty-Nine

The telephone rang several times and a hand reached over to grab it. The man lying in bed spoke into the receiver. "Hello." The voice on the other end was one that he had never heard before, but in his line of work it wasn't unusual for a new client to come looking for his services. "How did you get my number?" The voice explained that his organization was closely tied to Firewater and Blackwell, and that they had been very impressed with his previous covert operations around the globe. "I have no idea what you're talking about."

He sat up in bed and revealed a badly scared physique. His arms were covered with military tattoos and his chiseled chest and stomach bore a combination of bullet wounds and some sort of slash marks. "If you know me, then you know what to say." Mercenaries had to be careful. They never knew who might be calling. He had worked off and on for many years with every entity of the United States government, as well as the private companies that had infiltrated their ranks. Most of what he had done was well out of bounds for the US Constitution, but he always found a way to rationalize what he was doing.

The voice on the other side uttered, "Mongoose." This was the code he was given to assure that whoever was hiring him had talked to one of three, high level, United

States officials, in order to obtain his services. This gave him the green light, and meant immunity in case he was ever caught doing something that the written code forbade. People in his line of work lived by a different set of rules, and saw acts of torture and violence as a necessary evil on the path to preserve freedom. After he received his instructions, he slid out of the lodge pole bed, walked over to the window and gazed out of his log cabin.

He stood there, looking over the green, rolling pastures of cattle land as far as the eye could see. The noble, snow capped Grand Tetons were off in the distance. A dusty blond woman walked up behind him and wrapped her arms around him from behind squeezing tightly. "You have to go again?" He said nothing, he just nodded his head. "I thought you said you were retiring, that you wouldn't be going back over there." He turned around, and looked lovingly into her big, hazel eyes. "This one's a little different, it's domestic."

"Domestic? What?" She was more than a little concerned. "You don't work domestically." She was in love with this man and she never asked what his assignments were, but deep down in her gut she knew. She could feel that it was him every time some top level enemy of the state was assassinated. Yet, somehow she couldn't quite wrap her head around the idea that he was a killer.

"What's the assignment?" The words came, tumbling out of her mouth before she could stop herself. She had never questioned him before, but this was different. There was something wrong. She could see it in his eyes. He turned back to the window. "You know I can't tell you." She started to cry. "Wes, you're a good man and I love you. Please, please be careful. Don't do something that'll make you look like a monster." Her biggest fear, every time he went out on a mission, was that he would get caught and the government that he loved so much would leave him hanging out to dry. Conspiracy theories of the Oklahoma City bombing, 911 and the assignation of JFK went flashing though her brain. "Wes, turn it down. Don't do it, not this one. There has to be someone else that they can use." He said nothing, he just stood there watching a heard of antelope gallop gracefully through the distance. They never seemed to be swayed from their true course, always migrating with the changing seasons.

Chapter Thirty

Tiffany, was in the driver's seat and Brian, was riding alongside her on the passenger side of the Jeep as they veered onto the onramp, heading west. This was not the direction that Brian had been anticipating, but at this point he was done questioning. Something about this trip was pulling him, like he had never felt before. Everything seemed clear to him, like this was his destiny. Looking at Tiffany driving, he felt a sense of purpose and knew she was leading where they must go. For some reason he trusted her, and that was saying a lot for this playboy, who spent most of his young adult life avoiding meaningful relationships. In his usual pattern, he would meet a girl at the bar then go back to her flat to enjoy a night of passionate lovemaking and start over again the next night. Not that he treated these women in a negative way, but rather it was a mutual understanding that this was how things worked. He had no idea what life and love was really about. He was beautiful on the outside and therefore had come very far in life, but he was starting to become aware of the fact that something had actually been missing all along. Now he was sitting next to a woman that was exquisitely beautiful both inside and out, and he had no idea what to say, more importantly, that was OK with him.

Tiffany spoke loudly over the blowing wind and huge engine. "Aren't you going to ask where we're headed?"

"I imagine wherever your Dad wants us to." She smiled like Brian had never seen, it lit up her entire face, and he knew she also felt this trip was their destiny. She reached into the pocket of her dark red, Harvard sweatshirt and handed him the note. "Read it." He turned it over and read it to himself;

"My dearest Tiffany,

If you are reading this, then I am gone. There is so much that I wanted to tell you and show you, but it's not to be. What I have found will change the world more than any single event in history. I only hope that in saving it, it doesn't destroy you as it has me. Don't be angry or afraid, as I die knowing that your name will be on the biggest discovery in history;

Clue #2
Hidden in the Caverns of Knowledge,
at the end of the maze,
you'll find the key to unlocking everything.

Good luck and God speed,
Dad."

Brian turned to Tiffany. "I suppose you know exactly what and where he is talking about?" Tiffany turned to him and smiled, then nodded and looked back at the road. She and her Father had lived on a university campus in Gunnison, Colorado when he was going to graduate school. The school was called Western State College, and it was like a home away from home to Tiffany. Whenever she and her friends were able to play, they would make believe that the campus was a massive castle and that they were its royalty. She always played, "The Princess of the Caverns of Knowledge." So yes, she knew exactly where they were headed, and she even knew a secret entrance.

"Hey, can't they track these cell phones and your credit charges?" Brian asked. "When we pulled into Glenwood Springs last night, I went to Wal-Mart and bought two Go phones under a friend of mine's name, and I haven't used anything but cash."

"Do we have enough cash to get us where we're going?"

"You worry too much. I believe that I have a sufficient amount."

Chapter Thirty-One

Sandy ran into the hospital room, gave Ben a great big hug and kissed both of his cheeks. "Oh Ben, I thought I'd lost you." Ben, still groggy from the anesthesia, just grinned and lied back down. The Captain walked in, and Ben's eyes lit up. "Hey Cap, sorry about losing the suspect." The Captain just nodded and walked over to the bed. "You lost a lot of blood. How are you feeling?"

"I feel fine. Well, a little out of it from the drugs, but other than that I'm good."

"I don't want you out of this bed. Officer Tippet and Sandy will be assisting the federal agents on this one."

"Captain, those two, they didn't do anything. I was able to obtain a confession from one of the assailants before I had to kill him." The Captain looked at Sandy and back to Ben. "Kill, who did you kill?"

"I shot both of the guys that pulled a fake arrest on them." The Captain looked at Sandy. "Sandy, did they find any bodies?" She didn't flinch, "No, and the agents said it looked like the two were working together to escape." Ben sat up and looked at Sandy, then back at the Captain. "Something's not adding up Cap. I know I shot two men who had handcuffed our guys and taken them into custody. The blame is still being shifted to the lab assistant and the

Professor's daughter, who I know, had nothing to do with the death or my shooting."

"What are you suggesting?"

"I think this is some kind of cover up, maybe even a government conspiracy." Sandy laughed and the Captain smiled like Ben was out of his mind. "You need to get some rest." The Captain walked out of the room. Ben's voice was filled with urgency, "Sandy, you have to see that something's going on here." She tenderly grabbed Ben's hand. "Ben, I can't even think about the case. Ever since I saw you lying there, all I've been able to think about is you." Ben pinched himself, was he dreaming? He had known Sandy for years, and they were partners, but they had never crossed that line. Never in all their years together had he seen her so vulnerable.

Forgetting about the case for a moment, he allowed himself to gently place his hands on the sides of Sandy's cheeks. He pulled her face in close to his. "When this is all over, I will finish this." He planted a kiss right on her lips. It was a slow, passionate kiss, with feeling and emotion. It was the first time they had ever kissed each other, and for both of them it felt like fireworks were going off, they realized that they were meant for one another. Sandy filled with excitement, turned and ran out of the room. "I'll keep you updated."

Right then, a gorgeous, petite woman with wavy dark hair walked in and approached the bed. "I was listening to your conversation with the Captain. Do you really believe that there might be something going on?" Ben was suspicious of who this might be. "And who are you?" Then he recognized her and continued, "I know you,

you're that reporter, Ms. Levine. I have no comment." She was a smart and cunning reporter, and was not even close to giving up. "Look, your girlfriend there just assaulted me. But if I could find a better story, then I wouldn't need that one. It seems to me that we both have a stake at seeing this through."

Chapter Thirty-Two

As they drove through the high elevations of the Rocky Mountains, Brian and Tiffany remained silent. Although they had both been through the Leadville area and Independence Pass before, this time was different. The brilliant green colors of the Aspen trees seemed to jump off of their leaves and illuminate the expansive landscapes. The waterfalls seemed to glimmer like diamonds in the sun, and the wildlife never seemed so abundant. Suddenly, Tiffany slammed on the breaks and pulled over to the side of the road. She jumped out and hurried over to the embankment. Brian quickly followed her out of the Jeep without question. "Are we here?"

"No." Tiffany giggled. "I just wanted to show you something."

"Do we really have time?" She cut him off, "Brian, this could be our last day alive. We don't know, and you may never get the opportunity to see this again." Brian stepped closer to Tiffany and looked out across the valley. To their right, there was a waterfall that looked to be at least three hundred feet in height. The water was crashing violently down the mountain side. To their left, was a steep, rocky valley that looked as though it was still untouched by man. It was hard for Brian to imagine anything more beautiful. Tiffany pointed out in front of them. "Can you see that shape out in the distance?" Brian wasn't sure, "Which one?" She leaned in close to him so he could follow her fingertip to the correct spot.

Instead, Brian found himself slowly smelling her hair, and taking in its calming aroma. Suddenly, a funny feeling came over his tongue, it started to tingle and his mouth began to water. Brian was speechless, something he had never experienced before. Not because of the beauty of the landscape, but rather the beauty of Tiffany. Finally, his eyes followed the curve of her shoulder, down her arm, past her elbow and through the delicate valleys of her olive skin, to her smooth manicured hand that was pointing at, "A castle?" Brian asked, quite surprised. Tiffany stepped away, breaking the spell. "Good guess. They call it Castle Peak. The first settler's of this area thought it was a castle, some even wrote poems and stories about it. But, it's really a natural formation of rocks that just gives the illusion of a castle. It's a favorite for hikers because it's a fourteener, a peak that's over 14,000 feet."

"Wow. How cool is that?"

"One time, when I was a little kid, my Dad brought us up here to go hiking. He told us stories of gold miners and Indians...something I will always cherish." She turned and walked back to the Jeep.

Chapter Thirty-Three

Wes entered the small walk-in closet in his bedroom and shut the door behind him. The fragrance of cedar filled the tight space. He reached down to the left and pushed on a tie hanger that was attached to the wall. It tilted downward and made a clicking sound. He reached up and pushed on the back wall. The wall opened up, revealing a large storage area filled with weapons and ammunition. He walked in and grabbed one of his many Pelican cases from under a workbench. Nearly everything in the room was made of stainless steel, except for the weapons and a few random items. The space looked like a strange cross between a commercial kitchen and a high tech arsenal. The assortment made it appear that he was preparing for a war.

He pulled two Sig Sauers with silencers off of the wall and checked to make sure that they were functioning correctly. First, pulling the slide then checking the chamber. For Wes, these German made guns felt like an extension of his own body. He always hated the Glocks used by the military guys. Next, he pulled a black tactical vest off of the wall, he double checked to make sure that his holster and medical kit we securely fastened. Several loaded magazines, ready to insert at a moment's notice were also attached to the vest. He opened the Pelican case and lifted out a false bottom from each side. On the left side, he placed the two Sig Sauers and the tac-vest into custom compartments made just for them. On the right side of the suitcase, there were still a number of openings. He grabbed an H&K, PSG1snipers rifle, and began to break down the modular gun. It broke into seven small pieces that fit into their own empty compartments. Finally, he reached into a bin and removed a small, plastic box that was labeled, "C4". He opened the box and pulled out two rectangular chunks of what looked to be gray modeling clay. Wes liked working with C4, it was very stable, and therefore extremely easy for him to transport on his various missions. He wrapped each piece with wax paper and then placed them into their respective compartments in the case. Next, he reached into an open box labeled, "Switches & Timers" and pulled out two very different looking pieces of electronic equipment. After checking to make sure that they both worked, he placed them in the case. Finally, he packed a seven inch long combat knife with a leg holster. He then replaced the false bottoms in the case, and locked them in place. For all intensive purposes it looked like he had an empty suitcase. All he had left to do was pack some clothes and miscellaneous toiletry items. Then, most people would never suspect that under his disorganized packing job, existed a small arsenal.

Chapter Thirty-Four

"What are you talking about, assaulted you?" Lily knew from his tone, that he was hooked. She had been manipulating men for years, both professionally and personally. She knew from the anger in Sandy's eyes earlier and the concern in Ben's right now, that there was something between the two officers, even if they didn't know it themselves. Knowing this, she could use it to help her get the story that she really wanted. This was a story that could launch her into super stardom, and make her a national news personality.

"I asked her a couple of questions about the case and she came unglued. She hit me and took me to the ground. We have the whole thing on tape." Ben, not one to believe without seeing, demanded proof. "Let me see the tapes." She promptly turned around and walked out of the room. Then, returned in a few seconds with a portable video player and screen. She handed it to him, "Here's a copy, as you can see she was very upset." He pushed play and watched the video in silence, realizing that Sandy had indeed lost it, and put her future in jeopardy. If "Prime Time Levine" ran this story, Sandy would lose her job. She may even be demoted to traffic cop, which was worse than being fired.

Ben sat up. "OK. Here's the deal. I have a theory, and I'm willing to share it, if you give me the tape right now. Otherwise, we won't have any trust, and I can't work with someone who I can't trust." Lily, not one to throw away a good story was obviously reluctant, but at this point in her career she had to make something happen and this might be her last, best chance. At thirty-four years old, and still working the local news in a small market, she was already over the hill. Younger, prettier girls were coming out and moving up much faster. She just couldn't understand why she didn't make the cut. She had done everything right, given up most of her integrity, and even offered herself to some of the network guys, hoping to get the call up. That call never came. More than ever, she wanted to do something that was real. No more stories about Hooters employees or local construction workers not working hard enough. This was her chance and she knew it. "I tell you what Officer Lovato..." He interrupted, "Please, call me Ben."

"OK. Ben, you can have the tapes, but I need some information and your expertise if this story is going to be broken." Ben had no hesitation, because he too was not satisfied with his position in life and this case represented something he longed for, validation. "Let's get started."

Chapter Thirty-Five

Back at the station, the Captain and Sandy were sitting in on the federal agents briefing. The agents tried to give the impression that they had everything under control. The Captain could see right through their smoke screen and raised his hand, "Have you caught your tails yet?" The head agent didn't take kindly to such a blatant show of disrespect. "Look Captain, if you feel like you've got some suggestions on how to find our suspects, then you're more than welcome to give them to us." Not one to be shy, he answered back swiftly, "We need to run a trace on their cells."

"We did, and found their cell phones on the side of I-70, heading west."

"OK. So, we know which way they're headed. What about what they're driving?" The agent looked at his two counterparts, "Any idea of what they're driving?" The other two agents looked at one another then shrugged their shoulders. This made the Captain beam inside, but he was too proud of a man to rub it in their faces. "I was talking to Officer St. Claire, and she seems to feel like they might've taken a vehicle from the house that's next to the cabin. With a little luck, whatever type of vehicle it is was registered to the owner of the cabin." This immediately started the wheels turning.

"You heard the man. Find out what kind of car they're in, then we'll set up a road block at all possible routes out of the state." Now, the Captain was feeling more comfortable and confident. "They may be headed for one of the small mountain towns as well." The lead agent was surprised by the Captain's insight. He had worked on many cases, and he had yet to work on one where the local police had any clue what was going on. Here was a man who understood police work, but unfortunately was relegated to working in a small town. He felt sad that his skills weren't used to the best of their ability. This was the typical condescending view that made "Feds" such a dirty word to police across the country. They have a reputation for shutting down local investigations in order to prove who really holds the power. Many of the nation's best police officers are nothing in the eyes of these elite forces.

Today, the Captain showed his remaining officers that they belonged at the table. He demonstrated the true character of a leader. His coolness under pressure and confidence lifted the spirits of all that he commanded. As the meeting came to an end, he spoke to his troops, "I just want to remind you guys that we have a man down, and our window of opportunity is closing fast. So let's get to it."

Chapter Thirty-Six

"What do you mean get started?" Lily asked Ben, and he explained, "Well, we have to lay out a time line, and sequence every event that we know of. Then, we try to anticipate the next move. With a little help from Sandy and the guys, we should be able to get to them before anyone else, but we have to get started." He had her full attention. "So, what do we need?" He wasn't use to being in charge, but he felt an immediate surge of adrenalin and self confidence. "First, you need to get as many sticky notes as you can swipe from the nurses' station. We also need something to write with, dry erase would be great, some food and some coffee."

She jumped up and hurried out of the room. Ben exhaled a large breath, as if to let out the pain that he was holding back, then he sank back into his pillow. *What am I doing? How is this going to help anything, for all I know these two are involved somehow? What if this all turns out badly?* Before he could finish convincing himself that this was the wrong thing to do, Lily Levine walked back through the door with everything he had requested. "One of the perks of being a reporter."

"What do you mean?" She smirked and looked at him with her huge brown eyes. "I say jump, most people say how high." Her arrogance was one of the reasons she had failed to rise up the corporate ladder, and it was painfully obvious on this occasion. Ben was taken aback, "Must be nice." He rolled his eyes. She was unaware of the sarcasm in his response. "It is." Not wanting to continue the charade, Ben decided to change the subject. "OK. So, let's start with writing out a time line. Use the Expo pen on the floor. The linoleum should work just like a white board. The first event occurred at 9:00 A.M., when Professor Burt Gerardo, was assassinated at the REMRSEC natural energy lab, on the School of Mines campus."

Chapter Thirty-Seven

Sitting in a sleek, black, leather chair, surrounded by a dark mahogany desk, a young woman answered the phone. "Hello, Mr. Gildman-Cash's office. How may I help you?" After a brief silence, she reached over to touch a button then spoke back into her head set, "Mr. Cash will be right with you Ma'am." She pressed the hold button on the phone, then opened the intercom and spoke to her boss, "Sir, I have a lady on the phone who will not identify herself other than Virgin Mary. She is insisting that you take the call. Do you want me to get rid of her?"

"Did you say Virgin Mary?" She was embarrassed that she had even brought it up. "Sorry to have bothered you. I'll take care of it Sir..." He cut her off mid sentence, "No, no let her through." The secretary was fairly new and in these tough economic times she was terrified of doing something that may cause her to lose her job. She had good reason to fear this, unemployment in the United States had topped twenty percent, and big corporations were firing workers at the middle and low end of the salary range. Some accountant had figured out, that they could fire all of their secretaries with ten or more years of experience, and hire new ones in their place for half the money. They saved Gildman-Cash millions of dollars. The person she replaced, had worked for twenty-five years, and was let go for that very reason.

In her paranoia, she would often listen in on her boss's phone calls, trying to get any information she could use as leverage to insure her job. On this day, she was curious and had to listen. When he picked up the phone, she clicked off the line only briefly then she turned it back on to listen. "The ball is in play." Mr. Cash spoke into the receiver, "Are you serious, how is that possible?"

"You need to prepare. Someone found the final artifact and all five were activated. It is time for the final step." He turned around and stared out over the Manhattan skyline. "How long do we have?"

"Best case scenario, it will be at least a month before we start to notice any significant physical and mental changes. However, if our operatives can't locate and neutralize everyone currently involved, we could be talking martial law by Wednesday." Mr. Cash fully understood and grasped the enormity of the situation. "Who's on this one?" He had worked with all covert aspects of the government. Therefore, he was well aware of the fact that they were not above using mercenaries to help destabilize any region that wouldn't accept loans from its parent organizations or any other entity that threatened their power. "You know that I can't tell you that. It's better that you don't know, plausible deniability."

"Thank you for the call. Please keep me informed." He hung up the phone and sank into his huge executive chair. On the other side of the immense doors sat his secretary, utterly shocked by what she had just overheard.

Chapter Thirty-Eight

Pulling into Gunnison in the late afternoon, Brian could see why this picturesque, small mountain town had made it through all the ups and downs that decimated so many other communities. This valley held something different. "A wholeness." Tiffany said, as if she was reading Brian's mind. "What? What do you mean a wholeness?"

"This area has that elusive wholeness that gives it its life."

"How did you know what I was thinking?" Tiffany didn't even realize that she was answering questions, which hadn't even been asked. "I was just stating that this area has a wholeness that sustains life. It also has a unique geographic location that separates it from other areas." Brian, said nothing, but his thoughts were racing. *Is she reading my mind or is something else going on here? How is it that she knew what I was thinking? This has been the strangest twenty-four hours of my life, and yet here I am. There's something intriguing about this woman.* He stared at Tiffany, pondering how strong she seemed to be. She continued to look forward pretending not to feel his eyes glued to her slightest movement. In the past, she would have asked why he was staring, but not this time.

Something was different, she couldn't put her finger on it, but something was different.

A road sign for Western State College, pointed north off of the two lane highway they were driving on. Tiffany didn't turn and Brian didn't know the difference. She still hadn't filled Brian in on what they were doing, or where they were going. They pulled into the downtown area. On the left hand side of the street there was a community park filled with green fields and bleachers. In the afternoons, it was usually packed with teams playing all kinds of sports. Today was no different, and the stands seemed unusually full for little league games. "Must be a championship, huh?" Tiffany smirked, "No. They just take their sports very seriously in Gunnison." It wasn't unusual at all for small mountain towns to pack any and all sporting events. "You should see a Mountaineer football game. More people attend the games than could possibly live in this small town."

Brian had a naturally athletic build, but wasn't the slightest bit interested in sports. However, anything that Tiffany talked about seemed to be the only thing in the world right now. The way the words rolled off her tongue, her brimming confidence was infectious. *This is the strongest woman I've ever met. How does she continue to go now, only two days after her Dad was gunned down?* The homes in the town made it look like they had gone through a time warp, the Victorian era mountain cottages hinted at the laid back lifestyle enjoyed by the residents of this gorgeous little town. Every house had a large front porch filled with potted plants and cozy little sitting areas. Nearly all of them were occupied by at least one person enjoying the fresh summer air. When they got to what seemed to be downtown, Tiffany turned right on Main Street and parked. "We're here."

"Where's here and why are we here?"

"The place that we need to go to will be a little hard to explore until later on tonight, they don't close until midnight on Sundays, so we need to kill some time. I'm thinking there's nothing better than blending in like a tourist and enjoying the beauty of this place."

"You mean the 'Caverns of Knowledge' are too busy right now?" She smiled and winked as she jumped out of the Jeep, "Something like that."

Chapter Thirty-Nine

Sandy came running, out of breath, into the Captain's office. "I think I found it. The guy that owns the main house is a friend of Professor Gerardo's. I contacted him, and he said that he has a blue Jeep parked under the car port. I called the boys up there, and there's no Jeep. So, I ran a DMV check and found a CJ7, 1985, registered to a Mr. Michael Downs."

"Great work Sandy. Put out an APB on the Jeep. It won't be long before we track 'em down." She didn't hesitate she picked up the phone and instructed someone on the other end of the line to follow through on the APB. Then, she hung up the phone. "Captain, where do you think they're headed?"

"I'm not sure, Sandy. I'm not sure." He put his hand comfortingly on her shoulder, "Have you talked to Ben?"

"I've been waiting until I had something to tell him about the investigation." As if on cue, the radio on her hip chirped in. "Sandy, this is Ben, do you copy?" Surprised and excited by the call, she grinned and said to the Captain, "Speak of the devil." Then, she reached down and pushed the talk button on the radio, "Ben, we were just talking about you."

"We've been running through the time line and need some info." Perplexed by the word we, Sandy and the Captain looked at each other questioningly, she chirped back, "Who is we?" There was a long silence on the other end of the radio. Ben just realized that including Ms. Levine in an ongoing investigation was highly unusual and could cost him both his job and his relationship with Sandy. Unsure what to say, he looked at Lily Levine for suggestions, she just shrugged her shoulders. "Are you still there Ben?" Ben replied, ignoring Sandy's prior question. "I've just been going over the time line in my head and thought I might be able to help."

"Well, we just found out that they're probably driving a CJ7, registered to a Michael Downs. Other than that, the suspects are still at large."

"What about the two guys I put down? Did you find anything on them?"

"Sorry Ben. There was no evidence of anyone else involved at this point." Ben was not used to being questioned on his integrity. He was both shocked and hurt. The idea of them not following through on what he had said happened, was very obviously a slap in his face and a blow to his pride. "I'm telling you guys, something else is going on here."

Chapter Forty

Pulling into Denver International Airport was nothing new for Wes. However, this time he was picking someone up, instead of catching a flight out. From miles away he could see the enormous white tents with multiple, protruding points that adorned the main hub of the airport. He could also see his favorite piece of art, which overlooked every car as they entered the busy terminals. The thirty-two foot tall, 9,000 pound bronco, with blue skin and fiery, red eyes caused quite a stir with some people. The sculpture had been commissioned by the city of Denver in 1992, to be completed by a well known New Mexico artist. However, it had taken sixteen years of battles and ultimately the death of its creator before the project finally had come to fruition, and its beauty could be known to all. For Wes, a lifelong Bronco's fan and believer in fighting for your cause no matter the price, this statue represented everything that Denver was.

When he pulled up to the curb, he was careful not to get too close. Last time he got too close to a curb, his fiancé had opened the door of his brand new Ford Mustang Hybrid, right into it. This caused a scratch that was devastating to Wes.

A beautiful, long legged, blond, in a sleek, black pantsuit opened his passenger door and sat down next to him, "You going to get my bags?" He was annoyed by her presumptuous attitude. "Is that my job?" Never one to feel much of anything, Rothchild just rolled her eyes and buckled her seatbelt. "Fine." Wes unbuckled his belt and got out of the car. He grabbed her bags and threw them into the trunk, then slammed it shut. He walked back around the side of the car, sat down again and slammed his own door. Then, he turned to Rothchild, "Look, I took this job before I knew you were involved. We are not partners, and there will be no monkey business, understood." He turned back around, put the car in gear and peeled out as they left the terminal. "What the hell are you doing? Are you trying to draw attention to us?" Wes understood that they were in the US, and quickly slowed down.

"I mean, it's been at least five years, are you really still mad at me?" She reached over and put her hand on his thigh. He quickly removed her hand, "Look, you have the details, and I'm here for work. So, where are we going and what is it we have to do?" Rothchild was use to people kissing her ass. She looked like a runway model on steroids. Her long, muscular physique and good looks were a helpful tool in the espionage game. However, it was a game Wes had played before. There was no way he was going to let her control this assignment. "I said..." She interrupted him, "I know what you said, OK. You want to know?"

"Yes." She reached into her large purse and pulled out a file folder, "We have two targets. They are in possession of some valuable national security related artifacts. If we are unable to neutralize the targets and return the artifacts, then we have authorization for a sleeper." Wes abruptly pulled off of the highway right outside of the airport, he slammed on his breaks. "What, a sleeper on American soil? How is that possible?"

"Look, I don't like it either, but all we have to do is neutralize the targets and retrieve the artifacts during the next forty-eight hours, and everything will be just fine."

Chapter Forty-One

Tiffany and Brian were walking through the campus of Western State College. The night air was chilly and refreshing. The campus resembled a ghost town at this time of night. "The key is making it to the entrance in between security rounds." Brian, aware of the consequences, just grinned, "Whatever you say boss." Tiffany ignored him and continued to walk briskly. They traveled up a steep hill towards the center of campus. Brian had no idea where they were headed, "How much longer? This hill is killing me." Tiffany turned back and smiled, "We passed it back there. We just need to find security first, and see where they're at in their rotation." Brian was puzzled, "We are looking for security why?" Tiffany giggled, "This campus has had the same security team since I was a kid, and they always do the exact same rotation at the exact same time. As long as they're down at the amphitheater, we're good for about twenty minutes."

Brian was sorry he had asked. The last thing he wanted to do was question or upset Tiffany. He sped up and walked right next to her, he looked over and she was completely lost in thought. Her hair was waving behind her as she brushed back some loose strands to join the rest. Her dark brown eyes seemed to glow in the moonlight.

Suddenly, she grabbed Brian and threw him up against a huge Cottonwood tree. She put her hand over his mouth. Then, she began passionately kissing the back of it. Brian had no idea what was going on, but was staring into her eyes as she pretended to kiss him, he felt a tingle. A speeding golf cart came screaming by them. On the side was the word, "Security." Brian had almost hoped this was her way of flirting, but to his dismay she was just playing it smart. As soon as they drove off behind the amphitheater and down the hill, she let go.

For that brief twenty seconds, Brian felt more emotion than he had ever felt in his entire life. Yesterday and today were days that Brian would have never imagined before he met her. Now, the closeness of this beautiful young woman in front of him, made him feel like he was somehow alive, aware, afraid and burning with a glow that he had never had before. "I'm sorry Brian. I didn't hurt you, did I?" Brian had no response. He was so entranced in her eyes he could say nothing. Tiffany put her fingers in front of Brian's face and snapped them, "Wake up lover boy." Embarrassed, Brian turned beet red and couldn't look her in the eyes. "Oh, uh, I was just thinking how well, how strong you've been the past couple of days. I mean with everything that's happened and all." Tiffany, knowing she had struck a nerve, stepped off of the gas and stopped pushing for once in her life. "Brian, I really wouldn't be able to do it without your help. You're a good person." His face perked up and he stood up taller. "OK. I take it, that's what we were looking for."

"Yep, we got twenty minutes, let's go." She turned and started to run down the grassy hill. Brian followed closely behind, as she slowed down in front what looked to be a Spanish mission. It had a red, terracotta tile roof, a bell tower and an ornately carved stone entrance. "A church?"

"Not quite, but some may consider the library a form of church. This is the Leslie J. Savage Library. It was built in the thirties during the Spanish Colonial Revival period, so you are close." Suddenly, the "Caverns of Knowledge" clue crept into Brian's memory. He excitedly yelled out, "I get it!" Tiffany, a very observant person replied, "Yes. Welcome to the 'Caverns of Knowledge'." They walked around back and up a short flight of stairs. She turned and looked both ways to see if anyone was there. Then, she stepped into the planter and over to a grate in the ground just to the side of the rear delivery door. It looked like a water drainage cover. She leaned down and lifted out the heavy grate then looked back up at Brian, "Are you coming?"

Brian walked over and looked down into a deep, dark hole, "Right after you." She looked at him, smiled and jumped in, disappearing from view, as there was little to no light outside. Brian was worried and whispered, "Are you OK?" Tiffany's hand reached out of the hole, signaling with her thumb pointing up. Brian reluctantly bent down and lowered himself into the hole. He felt foolish when he realized that it was barely deeper, than he was tall.

Tiffany struck a lighter and lit up the path ahead. She brushed the cobwebs aside and crouched into a small, damp crawl space, Brian followed reluctantly. Underneath the building there appeared to be a little more light than there had been outside. Brian could see that there was another hole on the other end that seemed to have an even brighter light shining through it. As they made their way through the endless rows of school desks and chairs covered in dust, it reminded him of a graveyard for furniture. Tiffany turned away from the second opening which Brian had thought they were heading towards. Instead, she entered silently into the darkness, Brian quickly followed in fear of losing her. She finally reached an area of desks that were arranged to form a maze. "I suppose these are the desks."

"These are the ones. We made this nearly twelve years ago, and I bet no one but my Dad has even been down here since." She walked him through the maze and knelt down at the far end next to a very strange looking cube. The markings were hard for her to place. They appeared to be Puebloan, yet it had other unrecognizable symbols as well. On the top face of the artifact was a large indentation in the shape of a star. One ray of the star was filled in with an odd looking smooth stone. There was a shiny, round object in the center of the star that did not appear to be from this planet. It was unlike anything Tiffany had ever seen before.

Chapter Forty-Two

"This artifact is going to change the world. How is that possible?"

"Just be patient Brian. We're involved in something much bigger than ourselves." They knelt down next to the object and carefully examined the strange cube. It seemed to glow in this dark space. Tiffany had never seen anything like it and her jaw was open, clearly signifying her amazement. This made Brian feel a strange sensation that he had never felt before, a sense of calm washed over both Brian and Tiffany. They placed their hands on their thighs and they each took a deep breath. Written on the wall behind the artifact was a message;

The artifact has an importance
that outweighs all other discoveries.

Clue #3
If you are you, then find the first key
where the Pueblo slept on cliffs,
and praised our true Father.

TSIVOT

Silence had overcome Brian once again. However, this time there was no uncomfortable feeling. Instead there was a spark, a feeling of power. He had become part of something extraordinary. It felt as if he was joining all the great names of the past, Galileo, Newton, Einstein, now the names of Gerardo and Brady would join them. For a brief second, Brian felt as if he could see a glowing light hovering around Tiffany. He turned away, not wanting her to think that he was being a "lover boy" again. Tiffany took a picture of the wall with her phone then turned towards Brian. "OK. Let's go." She reached out, grabbed the cube and checked to see how heavy it was. To her surprise, it was extremely light. So much so, that she almost fell over backwards. "Wow, that's really strange."

"What's that?"

"It looks like it's made from stone, but its weight is more like that of tinfoil, and yet, it's still extremely hard like diamond." Brian reached out and touched the cube to feel for his self.

Chapter Forty-Three

In a hotel room across town, at the quaint Water Wheel Inn, Wes and Rothchild were sitting there arguing about anything and everything they could think of. "How is it I'm gonna sleep with only one bed?" Rothchild looked at Wes with eyes that could pierce though steel. "I'm not sure we'll be here long enough to use the bed. But I didn't think you would mind sleeping next to an old friend. I promise I won't bite."

"First of all, I am happily engaged, and I certainly don't feel comfortable sleeping in a bed with another woman." Rothchild was disgusted, "You'll kill the innocent, but won't lie down with me. That's rich." She walked over and looked at a slightly unusual, satellite tracking device that was sitting on the dresser next to the television then picked it up. Wes recognized what it was at once. "So, we know where they're at."

"No. We know that the last time the cube was moved it stopped in this general area. As soon as they move with the artifact, then we'll know exactly where they're at."

"Is the tracker on?"

"They won't be here for a couple of hours."

"You have no idea when they're going to be here. For all you know, they could already be here." She put the device down on the dresser and walked over to him. She pushed him onto the bed, grabbed his hair and straddled his legs kneeling down on top of him. "Silly boy, we're in the middle of nowhere. No one knows we're after them. They're sitting ducks. Let's just…" She reached down and tried to kiss him. Wes had enough. He stood up holding Rothchild out in front of him with his strong hands. He gently placed her down on the bed. Then he walked over and grabbed the tracking device. When he turned the power on, he was stunned to see that the artifact was on the move, and already heading towards them on the way out of town.

Chapter Forty-Four

Mr. Gildman-Cash pressed the intercom button on the phone, "Dani, can I see you please?"

"I'll be right there Sir." She turned around towards the mirror as she stood up. The black skirt of her suit had ridden up exposing thigh high stockings that covered perfectly sculpted legs. She smiled into the mirror to reveal gleaming white teeth, pale blond hair and sparkling blue eyes as she reached down to adjust her pencil skirt. *Maybe I shouldn't have worn these for my first date with Tommy. But man, it's been so long since I've been on a date. I just want to… impress. That's enough, take a deep breath, he's not that scary.*

Dani took a deep breath. Then she reached down, grabbed the handle and opened the door. As she stepped into Mr. Cash's office, her nostrils filled with the smell of thick aromatic cigar smoke. The expanse of the office was impressive. All around her were items that looked rich and luxurious. To her left, there was a white, marble statue of a nude, Greek god. To her right, was a massive display of red, mahogany bookshelves, all neatly arranged with books that appeared to be rarely used, they adorned the wall, stretching from the ceiling down to the floor. The back of Mr. Cash's monstrous leather chair was blocking him from Dani's view. All she could see was a lingering cloud of smoke that was growing around his chair. Unable to see him, she was afraid to say anything, so she stepped timidly into the middle of the room, between the door and the huge, carved desk that looked like a relic from the Ming dynasty. "Well, Ms. Bradford, what are you waiting for?"

"I beg your pardon Sir. I'm not sure..."

"Look, if you're going to work for me, then you have to tighten up your human relations skills. Now, pour me a drink of the Louis Tres, over there on the wet bar. It's the cognac in the Baccarat crystal bottle that looks like a piece of art." Instantly, she recognized the shiny piece of artwork that stood out in the middle of several other bottles. "How do you like it Sir?"

"On the rocks of course." She gently lifted the bottle from its resting place. It was hard for her to imagine why a liquor company would use such an ornate design. After pouring the liquor over the ice, she bent down and took a whiff of the intoxicating liquid. The aroma filled her nose and made her body shiver. "How can you drink something so terrible?" She walked over to the desk. Apparently, Mr. Cash had no intention of turning around, as his chair was still billowing cigar smoke. "Sir, where shall I place it?" He reached his hand out from behind the chair. She handed the glass to him.

"OK. Ms. Bradford, I need you to call my driver and tell him to get the limo ready to go to the air base."

"Air base, where is the flight headed Sir?" She jotted down notes into her notebook. "Well Dani, the plane is going to take us to Colorado Springs." She did a double take at what she had just written. "Who is us, in the conversation?" For the first time, Mr. Cash swung his massive leather seat around and faced Dani. His eyes burned through her, "I'm going to need you to come along for a weekend business trip." She thought back to the conversation she'd heard earlier. A shiver went up her back, and she wasn't quite sure what to say, she knew that part of her job description was being able to leave at a moment's notice. Mr. Cash traveled often, and preferred for his assistants to be with him on most trips. However, the phone call earlier was really bothering Dani, for some reason she couldn't seem to shake it. "Dani, are you able to do your job or not?"

"No, I mean, yes Sir. No problem. I was just thinking about how I was going to let my date know that I have to stand him up."

"OK. Then, I'll have the limo driver take you home and you'll both meet me back at the hanger. Bring enough clothes for five days, just in case this thing ends up taking awhile." Fearful of losing her job, she had no choice, so she went along with the plan. She was hoping that she was just letting her imagination get the best of her.

Chapter Forty-Five

Standing, looking into her tiny closet and indecisively choosing outfits for the trip, Dani was also dialing her cell phone. "Come on Lily, answer the phone." One of Dani's best friends during college was now a reporter for NBC's, 9 News Denver. Seeing how she was going to be in Colorado Springs, she didn't see why she couldn't meet up with an old friend. The answering machine came on, "This is Lily Levine. I'm not available right now, please leave your name and number after the beep."

"Hey girlfriend, this is Dani. I know it's late notice, but I'm going to be in Colorado Springs this weekend. Some kind of business emergency for the banking industry. I thought we could get together. You have my number." She closed the phone and hurriedly finished packing. Then, she took one last look around her puny, rodent infested studio apartment, before walking out with a rolling suitcase behind her.

Chapter Forty-Six

Ben and Lily were both digging through the pile of papers they had gathered in front of them, trying to make sense of what was going on. "Where would they be headed?" Lily was frustrated with the situation, "I don't understand why they're running if they have nothing to hide."

"Sometimes in our system, innocence is not presumed. They may have the answers. They just don't know who to trust." Lily couldn't believe what she was hearing, "I've never met a cop, who would say that before."

"We're not all the way we're portrayed to be in the media. In fact, I would venture to say, that most police officers are intelligent, disciplined and decent human beings." Lily was now aware that he had taken it the wrong way. "Ben, it's just nice to know that you're more than just a badge." Ben blushed and tried to change the subject, "When you went to get a drink I heard your phone ring." Lily picked up her Chanel handbag and reached inside. She pulled out a sleek little Blackberry and looked at the screen. Her eyes opened wide and she smiled. "Looks like you got some good news."

"Yes. An old friend will be in town this weekend."

Chapter Forty-Seven

As the limo pulled up to the enormous curved hanger, Dani could not believe her eyes. Parked immediately to the right of the hanger, was Air Force One, the jet airplane that the President travels in. "Wow!" She didn't think that the limo driver was paying attention to her. "She's a beauty, isn't she?"

"Yeah, I never thought I would be so close to the President's plane."

"Well, your trip tonight will be quite an experience then. We're flying with the President himself."

"What? What are you talking about? How can that be?"

"Mr. Cash, is very good friends with the head of the treasury, Mr. Gregor. He has been asked to take this trip, along with the President and his financial advisors."

Suddenly, the small town girl from Iowa felt a very uneasy feeling in the pit of her stomach. Her hands began to get clammy and she felt a little dizzy. How was it that she had gotten herself into a job with this kind of connections? She could not fathom how she went from waiting tables at a greasy spoon diner, to jetting around the states with the most powerful man in the world.

Chapter Forty-Eight

As Brian lifted Tiffany out of the cement hole in back of the library, the cold night air gripped his lungs. Gunnison, was located at 10,000 feet in elevation, and even in the summer time, the night air was cold enough to burn with every deep breath. They walked down the stairs and turned right, heading off campus. Tiffany had the artifact securely hidden under her red, hooded sweatshirt. At first glance, she looked as if she was carrying a baby. As far as Brian and Tiffany were concerned, the cube was even more precious than a child.

Suddenly, a golf cart flew around the corner. "Hold it right there! This is campus security!" Tiffany and Brian both looked at each other then Tiffany took off running, "Follow me." She ran directly into one of the brick dorm halls and down the stairs. Brian franticly tried to keep up. The security guard had jumped off his cart, and wasn't that far behind. As they entered the basement, they ran straight through an open laundry room. The damp air smelled stale and there were linens and clothing hanging everywhere. "I hope you know where you're going." She had led them to the other end and back up the stairs. They flew out the other side of the building. To Brian's surprise, Tiffany made an abrupt halt. She grabbed a broom sitting nearby, then slammed the doors shut and put the long steel handle though the loops in the door's handles. Bam! The door smashed into the broom handle, stopping the guard in his tracks. He bounced off of the door and landed on his butt.

Tiffany turned and looked at Brian, "I love this place." Her smile, though brief filled Brian with a feeling of hope and excitement. She turned and started running, "You coming?" Brian didn't hesitate, he ran beside her. He was becoming acclimated to the altitude and cold night air. They ran through the parking lot and into the side yard of a yellow mountain cottage that backed up to campus. Tiffany leaped up two stairs by the side door with the grace of a ballerina.

Brian had never witnessed such a sight outside of sports, where it is common place to see an athlete in the zone. That place, where the mind lets go and actions become automatic. That place, where the athlete seems to be in a world of his own. Tiffany already knew that this was the time, but Brian was just beginning to see it. When they passed the front of the house, she veered to the left, jumping over two potted miniature Rose bushes. As she reached the front of the lawn, and a dark band running across the yard she turned back, "Jump the ditch." Brian nearly stepped into one of the irrigation ditches that crisscrossed every lawn in town. They were there for watering lawns and gardens. They continued running across a street and in between two very large fraternity houses, adorned with their Greek letters on the roofs. When they reached the backyard, Tiffany slowed down, "I think we lost him. Come on, we need to get the Jeep."

Chapter Forty-Nine

Wes turned to Rothchild his voice overflowing with resentment, "It's moving. Let's go get 'em." Rothchild relished in knowing more about the mission than he did, she smirked smugly. "What color is the dot?"

"The dot, what do you mean?"

"The way this tracker works," Rothchild said, as she stood up and grabbed it away from Wes, "is different from anything else we have ever used."

"How's that possible? We've worked with the military's best." Rothchild grinned and walked over to the window, looking out over the beautiful landscape of the tranquil mountain resort. She scoffed as she saw the waterwheel and bridge that looked like they belonged in a fairy tale. "The item we're after emits high levels of energy that are unique. The first level is orange on this screen, when it turns blue, the last of five keys have been installed, fully activating the artifact. That's where we come in. Our employer will only pay us, if we retrieve the artifact with all keys intact." Wes was more than a little upset by this, he turned and walked away fuming, "How long am I going to be stuck with you?" He spoke seething under his breath. She was not detoured, Rothchild turned to him, "Look, if we don't kill these two, and retrieve the artifact with all of the keys, then a sleeper will be released, killing everyone and everything, possibly starting a war with whomever they end up blaming."

"How long?"

"We have four days."

Chapter Fifty

As they pulled into the immense, curved hanger, Mr. Gildman-Cash came over to greet the limo as the vehicle came to a stop. The driver jumped out and hurried around to open the door for Dani. When she stepped out of the limo she was instantly concerned, her boss's face looked different for some reason, worried, maybe even terrified. "Dani, I'm very sorry that you're being dragged into this. If I'd had any idea…" Before he could finish, four armed guards marched over, one of them pushed his assault rifle into Dani's back, "Time to board."

"What the hell's going on? I want a lawyer." The four guards said nothing they just continued to push the group towards the rolling staircase that had been positioned up against the main entrance door of Air Force One. Mr. Cash turned to her, "Your US rights no longer apply, calm down and save your energy."

Chapter Fifty-One

Sitting in his hospital bed, Ben was massaging his temples and trying to concentrate. Suddenly, he sat up and a knowing grin came over his face. Lily looked at him with curiosity. "Look at the time line. At 9:00 A.M., a man was killed. By 10:00 A.M., the next morning, men posing as federal agents, and real Homeland Security agents simultaneously arrived at the dorms and the police station." He smiled and turned to her, "Do you see now, what I'm talking about?" She looked back at the time line not really knowing what to say. Honestly, she didn't understand what Ben was talking about. "I'm not sure I do see what you're saying."

"Have you ever taken a math class where you had to solve probability problems?" She looked at him and answered blank faced. "Yes."

"OK. Then, what are the chances that the two are unrelated incidences? I'm no math genius, but I'm pretty sure that it's highly unlikely. That leads me to believe, that it's probably connected. Maybe, the Professor was killed by someone with connections in the government at a very high level." Suddenly, the pieces fell into place. "Holy crap! I can't believe it. This Professor was working on some kind of new power source. This is about energy!" Ben smiled and continued, "Not only that, we've got two suspects out there, and they have something so valuable, that our own government is willing to kill for it." Lily looked at Ben, she was overwhelmed with emotions. The enormity of the situation had just hit her. She was feeling amazement, worry and exhilaration all at the same time. "What can we do?"

"Right now, we need to find them before the station does and leads them right into the fed's hands."

Chapter Fifty-Two

Brian turned to Tiffany and yelled over the wind inside the Jeep, "So, how many keys do you think this thing has?"

"I'm not sure, I think maybe five. The star on top of the cube has five rays and four of them are missing. Something has to go there. So, I kind of think we're looking for the other four pieces of the star. But, there is one thing that I know for sure, where the first one is located. My Dad's clue leads us to Mesa Verde National Park."

"Mesa Verde's a pretty large place, are you sure you can find it?" Tiffany just smiled and winked at Brian, "Have you ever heard of a group of Indians called the Puebloans?"

"Yes."

"Well, there's one school of thought out there that believes the Pueblo were an ancient alien colony that abandoned their dwellings to go back to the sky." Brian looked at Tiffany in disbelief. "I'm not saying it's true, I'm just telling you the legends of the Pueblo people. One group in particular, the Hopi." Brian looked up in astonishment, "Hopi? Did you know the research we were doing was on a new element we've been getting from the Hopi reservation in Arizona?"

"You said my thesis was the stuff of legends didn't you?" Brian shook his head in disbelief, "Yes. Yes I did."

"Well, if you read it, then you know, that I theorized our knowledge of engineering and geology, are just now starting to catch up with the achievements of past civilizations. Meaning, that archeology is an extremely important part of our future."

"And that's when you went to Harvard to study archeology, right?"

"That's right. Anyway, archaeologists have been finding evidence that some of these tribes and their ruins predate much of Western civilization. That means the timeline is off on most of our historical accounts. If this cube turns out to be what I think it is, it will change everything."

Chapter Fifty-Three

As Dani entered Air Force One, she couldn't believe where she was, she almost forgot how worried she had been. The group proceeded down the plane's hallway. On their left they passed a galley and a large, fully appointed conference room. They continued through a small workroom and finally emerged into the rear of the plane. There were neat rows of luxury, reclining seats, it looked like a typical first class passenger cabin. However, Dani was shocked to see that every powerful player in business and government was gathered there. As she walked, she smiled and couldn't believe she was in the company of former presidents Herbert Hyde Jr. and Sr., Clint Williams and more. President Tobiah, was somewhere on board the plane as well.

The guards led them to an empty row. "Here you are." Dani slipped into the seat at the end, next to the window. Mr. Cash and his limo driver, who also served as his personal bodyguard, sat down next to her. "Just keep your mouth shut, let me do the talking, and you'll make it out of this." Dani was fed up, "This, I don't even know what this is. How dare you involve me in something so dangerous?" Mr. Cash snapped back, "Look, we are on the precipice of World War III. Make it through, and you'll be compensated well. So keep your mouth shut."

"What do you mean World War III? How is that possible?"

"You'll find out more as the night goes on. Essentially, something has been found that could end our life as we know it." Dani didn't flinch, "Like what?" *What could possibly change life as we know it?* "The Point of Origin and the destruction of the world." Dani was completely lost she had no idea what he was talking about. "Which means what?"

Chapter Fifty-Four

"What do you think it is?" Tiffany was getting tired, so she pulled off of the road and stopped the Jeep on the shoulder of the mountain highway. She turned and looked at Brian, "I think it may be an ark." Brian was not sure what she meant, "What kind of ark? Like Noah's Ark?" Tiffany took a deep breath, "The Ark of the Covenant, Noah's Ark, the Holy Grail, these are simply metaphors, trying to explain unimaginable powers in something. You have to remember, many of the ancient accounts had much to do with the level of literacy the people had. Meaning, they didn't always know how to describe something that would eventually translate well into English."

"What are you talking about?"

"Look, the artifact may be a number of things, but my Dad's note hinted at something extraterrestrial, and referenced the Point of Origin. This can only lead me to one conclusion, that this cube is some kind of ark which played a role in human creation." Brian couldn't believe what he was hearing, "How can you bring creation into a scientific and historical find?" Tiffany smiled and put her hand on Brian's leg, "Silly boy, you may have heard my Dad say on many occasions, that science is the manifestation of man's need to figure out the Point of Origin. Modern science was actually created as a means to discover the truth of our existence." Brian nodded and she went on, "As we contemplate our journey tonight, I'm confident we have found the answers to some of man's most enduring questions. This little cube, or ark may just be the catalyst for mankind."

"Isn't it possible that it's the catalyst for some kind of power related to our research on the new element we've been testing? After all, your Dad just recently went down to Arizona to look for a sample of what we thought was a possibly a meteorite, we weren't sure. It was similar to the Chassignite meteor that had been found in France during the early 1800's, but it wasn't exactly the same. "

"It may have played a role in finding the artifact. But I'm just now starting to realize, that something down there scared him enough that he hid the keys and this cube, hoping that only I could find them. Don't you see? He found something that warranted splitting up the artifact and leaving clues which only I could follow. Whatever this cube holds, it's big, and there's nothing bigger than the Point of Origin. We're talking Big Bang, Evolution, Creation, all obsolete based on the findings we will publish." Brian could see her joy and felt no reason to remind her of the pain she had endured during the past few days. He just nodded and grinned, "I hope you're right." She started the Jeep with a newfound energy. "Time we get back on the road." Their hands were resting, one on top of the other as they pulled away. Brian felt as if she may have left an opportunity available, and decided to just be in the moment. Tiffany smiled and squeezed tightly as they drove off into the night.

Chapter Fifty-Five

Mr. Cash could tell that Dani was starting to get irritated. So, he decided to fill her in before she lost her cool, and brought any unneeded attention to him and his two companions. "Look, Dani, the thing is, at this level of business the lines we thought we would and wouldn't cross start to get blurred." She turned and looked away, he continued, "How familiar are you with the New World Order?" Surprised, she turned and looked at him. "The NWO is real, well the general idea is, but we go by another name and purpose. Many have been misled into believing that our organization is driven by race or politics. In reality, money is our only true motivator and connection to one another. Tonight, we are meeting to deliberate the future of the world as we know it."

"How is that possible? I thought only crazies and lunatics believed in that stuff." He put his hand on her knee. She could feel the plane vibrating as it began to move, he kept talking, "Dani, when you were hired we went to great lengths to find someone that had very few attachments, family, et cetera. You have just been given the key, to an amazing world. Play your cards right, we'll not only make it out of this alive, you'll never have to work again." She looked insulted and whispered back, "I get kidnapped at gunpoint and you want me to just play along.

What's to stop them from just killing all of us?" He could tell she needed more, "I assure you, what we will be part of tonight is more important than you and me. It's about human existence, and the beginning of the end." Her eyebrows raised and he knew he had her. "You're about to witness an ancient voting ceremony to determine the fate of the human race, and the verdict is anyone's guess."

"How can that be?"

"Tonight, you'll find out that many of the things you believe about this world are only what we wanted you to believe."

Chapter Fifty-Six

"We just received word, that a report was filed about a couple matching our suspect's description breaking into the Western State College library." The station was alive with action. The Captain was leaning over a large conference table, pointing at a map the two federal agents had brought in. It was a print out of the schematics for the greater Four Corners area. Agent Pope pointed at Gunnison, on the map, it was in the southwest corner of Colorado. "Our information leads us to believe that they are headed from here towards the center of the Four Corners area. We also think that they may have acquired a suitcase bomb that could yield a three to five kiloton blast."

Sandy was shocked, "These two don't strike me as terrorists, and why would they head to the Four Corners area? There's very little that a nuclear bomb would do to affect our country from that area." Agent Pope was cocky and answered with confidence, "A suitcase bomb detonated near the Colorado River would be a silent killer. Effectively, the entire Southwest, and the world would be affected considering the farming that relies on that water." The Captain decided to intervene, "How 'bout we concentrate on finding them, and then worry about scenarios afterwards."

Sandy looked at the agent and nodded, but with a hint of reservation. This sounded way too farfetched for her. She had gone to college at the School of Mines. She'd had Professor Gerardo as a teacher. His daughter often spoke in his classes as a guest, and neither of them even closely resembled what you would think of as a terrorist. However, this was her job and her boss was right. The faster they found these two, the faster they would know what was going on.

Chapter Fifty-Seven

Dani was now intrigued by what Mr. Cash was implying, she leaned in close to him, "And what is it that we're supposed to think? How is it possible that tonight is so important?" Mr. Cash was now a little annoyed. "Someone found something that will expose the truth about our existence. We knew it was out there, but we had no idea where." She interrupted him, "Then how do you know, that it was found?"

"This special artifact has four identical replicas that have been discovered over the course of history. We have gone to great lengths to keep their secrets hidden. Last week, when the fifth one was activated, it in turn activated all four others. Together, they act as a beacon, or a distress call to the stars. We were able to locate one of the men who found the artifact, but not until it was too late."

"Too late, too late for what?"

"We believe the signal was unable to breech our global filter and call our creators to us."

"What do you mean creators?"

"I can't really tell you, because I don't know completely. What I can tell you is that there is still hope."

"Hope, none of this makes any sense. How can you tell me that there's hope when you said that mankind's fate will be decided tonight?"

"If we can find the artifact, and keep the information contained, then World War III will be postponed."

"World War III?" Her shoulders sank and she scowled, he continued, "I am not at liberty to elaborate, but you will learn a lot tonight, if you stay with us." He said it as if she had a choice, and in a way, she did have a choice. If she played nice, she would be allowed to hear some of mankind's greatest secrets. On the other hand, if she made a scene, she got the feeling that she may not make it through the night alive. "How can you possibly think that I can sit here and let you tell me all these things, and not expect me to just blow this whole thing open." He looked at her with a very stern face, "Dani, tonight you'll be given the choice, join or die. This is not an idol threat. As long as you follow my lead, and things work out with the artifact, life will continue as is." She was shocked, her life was in danger. "How will the artifact thing work out?"

"There are a couple of terrorists trying to locate the pieces needed to activate the artifact. They have no idea what kind of hell they are unleashing on the human race. As long as they are neutralized before it is exposed, our world will continue status quo."

Chapter Fifty-Eight

Sandy was standing inside of the dark, cramped supply closet again. The smell of lemon scented cleaner filled the air. "Come on, pick up." The phone next to Ben's hospital bed rang again. Lily asked Ben, "Aren't you going to answer that?"

"Nobody knows I'm here that wouldn't call my cell first." Lily, not one to let an opportunity pass her by, looked directly at Ben and defiantly picked up the phone, "Hello, Officer Lovato's room." Ben was incensed and angry, now whoever was on the line would know he was working with someone. However, his mood rapidly changed after she began to speak, "This is his nurse, he's just returning from the restroom." She smiled and handed him the phone. "Ben, listen, I'm not sure how much time I have."

"Sandy?"

"Yes." she whispered. "Something is wrong, terribly, terribly wrong."

"What? What is it?" His look of concern worried Lily, but at the same time it also sparked the reporter in her, and a million questions ran though her head. "Slow down Sandy. What is so terribly wrong?" Ben tried to soothe her like he had done in so many other instances, but unfortunately this was different. Ben could detect it in her voice. "The feds..." she sighed, "...The feds are saying that our suspects are in possession of a suitcase bomb, and that they intend on using it. But it's the same guys you had in custody earlier. All I keep hearing running though my head, is you saying that something else was at play."

Ben could not believe what he was hearing. His pulse began to race with excitement. This was the case of a lifetime, his entire demeanor changed. Lily sat inquisitively watching the whole event slowly unfold in front of her eyes. Ben sat up straight for the first time since surgery. He barely flinched and his face was very serious, "Sandy, listen to me very carefully. You need to get control of yourself. If what you are saying is true, then I need you to stay focused. I need you to be my eyes and ears as this one unfolds. There's no way those two are terrorists. This is a set up. Something else is at play. Just get me as much information as possible." Sandy was leaning up against the back wall of the closet, with her head dropped down in front of her, "Ben, what can you do, in your condition?"

"This is a time that calls for great sacrifice, and I think I can endure some pain to do my job to protect and serve." Although Sandy wasn't completely convinced, she played along because she loved Ben. The last couple days, had made her understand that more than ever. Ben continued, "Is there any idea of where they're headed?"

"We just had a report, that a couple matching their description was headed to the Four Corners area leaving Gunnison. But that's it, that's all I know for now."

"Alright Sandy. Hang in there. I'm headed that way. Call me on my cell if you find anything out, or hear anything new. Leave a message cause some areas out there don't have cell coverage."

"You can't go out there by yourself. What is it that you think you can do?" Sandy began to frantically question the situation, and Ben tried to ease her worry, "Look, I know exactly what to do. Just keep me informed and I'll be one step ahead of the agents." She sighed, "…Ben, I love you." A warm smile filled his face, "I love you too." They both hung up the phone.

Chapter Fifty-Nine

Dani looked down at her knock off Prada handbag. *I'm so out of place here.* She reached in and pulled out her cell phone inconspicuously. Her phone had an audio recorder built into it, and she had an idea. "Mr. Cash, I think I see what you're saying, but I just want to make sure I have it straight. You're saying that if the two fugitives you're seeking are killed, before revealing the secrets an ancient artifact holds, then our world will be fine. But, if you don't succeed, then you and your friends here will start World War III, by detonating a suitcase bomb on them?" Mr. Cash was not amused, "First of all, that is only part of the story. Second of all, if you don't keep your voice down, they'll kill all three of us. Do you understand that?" He was visibly angered, and turned away, but she had what she wanted. Now all she had to do was wait until landing. Once the plane was in Colorado Springs, she could send the recording off to Lily, the only person she felt she could trust at this point. *Maybe, just maybe, she can get this out to the people.*

Chapter Sixty

Rothchild was visibly upset, "I can't believe we're not going to stay the night." She dug through her Louis Vuitton duffle bag for something. Then she zipped it closed, tossed it in the trunk and slid into the passenger seat of Wes's Mustang, "You know your inability to land a woman might have something to do with your aversion to sleeping in a bed, mountain man." He looked at her, shook his head and started the car. "You know I'm engaged. I wish you could get over yourself." Rothchild was disgusted, "I suppose you think we're sleeping in this piece of shit?" Wes just laughed, "I'll do whatever it takes to stay on the trail of our prey. There's no way, on my watch a nuke will be dropped on this great country."

"Your allegiance to this country is so childish. You're a killer for hire, just like me... married that's funny." Wes had had enough he elbowed Rothchild right on the chin, instantly knocking her out. *I thought you'd never shut up.* Rothchild looked at Wes, who was sitting there staring off into space, "Hello. Is anyone home? Let's go." Wes shook his head as he snapped back to reality, "Sorry, just daydreamin'."

"Whatever let's just go." He pulled out of the parking lot and followed the direction indicated on the tracking device. As he started driving down the highway, he started to think aloud, "I can't believe it, how is this possible? If we don't succeed, we're gonna let a sleeper loose on our own soil. I remember when 911 happened. People accused the government of being involved. I didn't think that they would be so directly involved with something that would kill so many Americans. I mean, I know it happens in other places, but here? Now, I just don't know what to think."

Chapter Sixty-One

Ben turned and looked at Lily he could see the excitement in her eyes, before he had a chance to say anything the reporter in her pounced, "Terrorist? What is…" Ben looked at Lily, and interrupted her, "Listen Lily, I don't have time to explain right now. Do you have a vehicle here?"

"Yeah, my mobile studio is outside right now."

"As soon as we're on the road, I'll tell you about everything. But I need you to get some more of these saline bags for my IV, to keep me hydrated. I'll meet you out front." Lily didn't hesitate she turned and walked purposefully out of the door. Not exactly sure how she was going to get the bags, she couldn't hide her eagerness. Her mind was searching through all of the different possibility's tonight had presented. Her time had finally come to prove that she belonged in the journalism world. Not for her stunning good looks, but for the substance of her stories. She nearly broke into a skip before turning the corner. Ben meanwhile, was getting partially dressed, collecting all of their notes and copying the time line off of the floor for the road trip.

Chapter Sixty-Two

The sun broke over the eastern horizon, sending a flaming glow across the vast landscape of the Southwest. The first rays of light beamed off of the side mirror, hitting Brian right in the eyes. He rolled over in the passenger seat onto his other side and shivered, he was quite cold. He slowly opened his eyes and to his surprise, Tiffany wasn't sleeping in the seat next to him anymore. He sat up quickly to survey where she may have gone. His mind was rapidly set at ease, when he looked back towards the sunrise and he saw her unmistakable silhouette. She was perched up on the hill doing a yoga pose, called the Tree. The sunlight engulfed her, and her shape resembled the rising of the Phoenix, in all of her glory.

Brian took a deep breath and grinned. His heart had filled with that unfamiliar feeling again. There, on a plateau in the Southwest desert, Brian had an epiphany. The world stopped, as he turned to get out of the Jeep. Every inch of the landscape exuded a brightness of color that he had never seen before. A glistening drop of dew, dripped off the extended leaf of a Yucca, as he turned to walk towards Tiffany. The fine, red dirt sifted between his toes as he slowly approached the most beautiful sight he had ever seen.

As he approached, he heard something that immediately changed his prior objective. Tiffany, standing in the Tree pose, was weeping. Her strength only went so far, and Brian wasn't sure what to say or do. So, he decided to turn around and leave, but in the process he stepped on a branch, snapping the silence and awaking Tiffany from her weeping meditation. "Brian, did I wake you?" He couldn't see her face yet, as she stood in the sun's path. "No. Are you OK?" She turned around and put her leg down, then walked towards him and gave Brian a great big hug. She put her head right on his chest and went back to the weeping. She squeezed Brian tight, as he returned the favor.

After sixty seconds, Tiffany spoke, "Brian?" He looked down at her, "Yes?" She peered up into his clear blue eyes, "Why are you still here? I mean, you could've left. And what if this…" Brian knew she just needed to be reassured, so he interrupted her, "Tiffany, I'm here because I want to be. First of all, I want to be part of the world's greatest discovery. And then, well, there's this, well, I just feel like you may need help." He blushed and smiled looking up across the mesa. "Is the park open yet?" he tried to change the subject. Feeling his embarrassment, she let go of him and answered, "No. The park opens at 8:00 A.M."

"Do you know exactly where to look for your Dad's next clue?" She turned and walked over to the edge of the plateau, looking down over the desert. He walked up beside her. "Well, I'm pretty sure it's in the Sun Temple based on his clue."

"Why?"

"In the clue, he referenced the place where the Pueblo praised our true Father. The Hopi believed that the sun was our Father, so if we're going to Mesa Verde, then the Sun Temple makes sense to me."

"What is it we're looking for?" She turned her head and looked up at him, "That, I honestly don't know, but when I see it, I will."

Chapter Sixty-Three

Sandy walked into the station's conference room, where they had set up their central hub for the investigation of Dr. Burt Gerardo's death and its ties to terrorism. Agent Pope hovered over his partner, Agent Swanson. However, Agent Swanson was clearly the one in charge. He was intent on finding the suspects. He leaned over the map placed on the large meeting table, his hands and arms supporting most of his weight. The room was filled with smoke swirling around. Everyone seemed to have a cigarette hanging out of their mouth. The Captain, who was leaning back in his chair, sat across the table from where Agent Swanson was peering down at the map. He broke the silence, "So, how is it that these two have gone from model citizens to terrorists in a matter of twenty-four hours?"

Agent Swanson had no patience for incompetence. "Look Captain, I know you may not understand the whole chain of command thing and clearances and all, but we have classified evidence that proves her Father was a terrorist, and that she had the same leanings. If I could, I would share it with you. But for now, let's just catch them and then well sort it out in court later." The Captain knew not to confront this little, round man who was vertically challenged and had an ego large enough to make up for what he lacked in stature. So, he used his best human relations techniques to steer the conversation in a better direction. He grinned, "I understand and agree, let's catch these guys." He stood up and joined Agent Swanson in staring at the map.

Chapter Sixty-Four

The Mesa Verde guide was wearing the recognizable Stetson style hat and olive green adorned by park rangers all over the country. Brian and Tiffany had signed up for the tour of the Cliff Palace and the Sun Temple. They had already been to the impressive cliff dwelling. It was truly amazing. An entire pueblo had been built on the side of a palisade striated with various orange hues. The only access was by a series of wooden ladders that climbed the sandstone cliff wall and then spread throughout the complex like a spider web. The ancient Pueblo people would carry water from the valley floor below in pottery on their heads as they ascended the ladders. The Cliff Palace lived up to its name, with its panoramic view which was truly regal.

Now, they had finally arrived at the Sun Temple. It was a minor structure in stature, compared to the Cliff Palace that they had just explored, however its purpose was much grander. The temple had been built by the Bow Clan of the Puebloans and therefore was erected in the semi-circular shape of a bow. What remained of the once towering, adobe brick, temple walls, were now nestled between large, noble Junipers. Throughout the tour, the guide had explained numerous other facts about this breathtaking and unique national park, but what she just said made the hair on the back of Brian's neck raise when the words came out of the her mouth. Tiffany, had a similar reaction, but more sublime and affirming, it was her Father leading the way.

"Here we are. The Pueblo People believed that the sun was their Father. This is where they worshipped him. Please be respectful when entering the temple, and please don't vandalize this national treasure. As you will see in the room in the southeast corner, someone decided it was OK. It's too bad, because they may not let people see these places anymore if we don't respect them." Brian looked at Tiffany and didn't have to say a word. They headed straight for the room that had been vandalized. When entering, they both had to duck through the square opening that was two feet off of the ground, and served as the door. They entered into a small room that had laid brick walls, with a layer of smooth adobe still covering them in places. On the right hand wall was an opening leading to another room, on the wall to the left was a barrier of caution tape and a handmade sign, asking people not to carve on the temple. There was an arrow pointing at a sequence of numbers, variables and a phrase;

Clue #4
"Point of Origin"
AD -8/3x – 54 (-19, 4)
Under the concrete rainbow lies the key.

PEPT

"This is it." Brian looked at her in wonderment, "Are you sure, what does it mean?" Tiffany took out her phone took two pictures, turned and said, "Let's go."

"What if...." She put her finger on Brian's lips, turned and walked over to the door, "You coming?" She ducked out of the room, Brian couldn't help but grin. He quickly followed her. She walked straight up to the guide, "Ma'am." The guide turned, "Yes. Is everything OK?" Tiffany put on a sad face, "How much longer is the tour? I need to get to the car, I'm not feeling well."

"This is the last stop. We'll be back in about ten minutes."

Chapter Sixty-Five

Tiffany and Brian were sitting in the Jeep, in the main parking lot where the tour van had dropped them off. They were looking at the pictures of the clue they had just found. Brian was drawing the clues onto a piece of paper. *What could this possibly be?* He looked out the corner of his eye to see if the expression on Tiffany's face would indicate any thought she may have had. He could instantly see that she was frustrated. "To me, it looks like gibberish." There was a hint of defeat in her voice. Brian sat up straight and placed his hand on her shoulder, "It's OK. Let's get something to eat at the store we saw on the way in. Then maybe, look at the clue again afterwards from a different perspective."

She started the Jeep and pulled out of the parking lot and onto the road. As they drove, silence took over Brian again, but this time it felt different. The sound of the Jeep, the wind blowing in his hair, adrenaline filled his heart with hope and excitement. The beauty of the Mesa Verde area came alive before him. The Junipers seemed to be greener than usual. The red, clay soil sparkled in the distance, glistening with the luster of ruby jewels. The smell of pine filled his nostrils with nature's glow. The exhilaration overtook him in a way that touched every inch of his body from his toes to his nose. He gazed at Tiffany on his left, driving the car. The background faded into blurs of light and color. Her essence filled his world, and he knew he had never seen anyone so beautiful. Not just physical beauty, this woman was the total package. Here, today, Brian could see her unlike anyone he had ever seen before.

Suddenly, his attention was broken when the Jeep bounced as they entered the parking lot of the general store at Mesa Verde. They pulled up in front of the store and parked. Tiffany turned off the Jeep. "Coming?" She jumped out. Brian grabbed the backpack and the drawing he had made of the clue. They went into the store and bought prepackaged sandwiches and fountain drinks.

On their way out to sit on the benches in front of the store, they were stopped by a young Indian boy. He had long dark hair that hung, loosely in his face and big brown puppy dog eyes. "Can I do a card trick for you?" Tiffany loved kids. She turned to Brian and smiled warmly, "We're going to sit right over there. Why don't you come over and show us while we eat." The boy smiled back, "OK." They all turned and walked over to the picnic tables and sat down. Tiffany introduced herself and Brian to the boy, "I'm Tiffany. This is Brian."

"I'm Sequoia." He held out the deck, "Pick a card." Tiffany reached out and chose a card. Brian eagerly peeled the cellophane wrapper from his tuna sandwich and took a bite. Sequoia continued with his trick, "Take a good look at the card and then show it to Brian." She looked at it. It was the seven of clubs. She showed it to Brian who nodded with approval as he chewed and swallowed down his first bite. Tiffany placed the card back inside the deck.

Then, he asked her to shuffle the cards. She shuffled then handed the deck back to him. Sequoia placed it on the table and asked her to split it into five equal stacks. She did as asked, and he took the top card off of each stack. He placed the five cards in front of her then asked her to check and see if her card was one of them. Tiffany picked up the stack, looked through it and smiled, "Nope." He continued smiling, "Great. Now, put the cards back down in front of you." He turned to Brian, "Could you please, now flip over each card in front of her one at a time?" The first four, were obviously not the card in question. Then, he asked Tiffany again, "Are you sure your card was not one of these five?"

"Absolutely." He smiled with confidence and asked Brian to turn over the last card. Sure enough, to Tiffany's surprise, the seven of clubs was there. "Wow! How did you do that?" He stood up, "A good magician never reveals his secrets." He looked down at the paper Brian had sitting next to the backpack, "Algebra." Brian and Tiffany looked at him and both asked, "What?" Sequoia pointed at the paper and repeated, "Algebra." Both of their eyes peered down at the paper. They both suddenly jumped up, Tiffany ran around the table and gave the boy a great big hug. "How old are you anyway?"

"Way too young for you." He giggled, "Really, fourteen." Brian took a twenty dollar bill and handed it to Sequoia, "You have no idea how much you just helped us."

Chapter Sixty-Six

Air Force One came to a stop on the runway of Peterson Air Force Base in Colorado Springs, just a short distance from Cheyenne Mountain. The complex housed many different facilities. The most well known of these was NORAD a multinational venture created during the 1950's in order to protect against outside threats. The complex was designed to withstand a thirty megaton blast within a mile and then self-sustain for an indefinite period of time. It was rumored to even contain its own water reservoir. This had led many people to believe that the complex also housed a secret bomb shelter for presidents and dignitaries.

Dani had remained quiet for the remainder of the trip, but in her mind she still had many questions. *How could this be the end? How is it that there'll be no one to miss me if I'm gone?* She felt as if she had left no mark, no lasting impression or contribution for this world in which she lived. She had not yet loved, not really loved, not the kind of love that endures all. She had never seen Europe. Her ideas and creations would never come to be. This saddened her greatly, but more than anything it strengthened her resolve. She would not let this happen. No one else deserved to die. She would not contribute to the ignorance, complacency and appeasement that existed.

Tonight, she would make her mark and people would remember her.

"Dani, Dani." Mr. Cash reached down and tapped her on the shoulder. She snapped out of her trance and grinned, "Sorry, just daydreaming."

"That's great. Now get up here." Dani looked out the window to see the majestic expanse of the Rocky Mountains with a glowing orange and violet sunset behind them. She turned to Mr. Cash, "Excuse me?" She snickered and gave him a look that could have frozen time, had he noticed. However, the arrogance of corporate executives has been well documented in the media over the past couple of years. They continued to grow rich and collect million dollar bonuses, all in the face of an economic meltdown that left millions of people unemployed. Dani had never met people like this before, and now was her chance.

As she walked through the plane's door she reached into her purse to grab her cell phone. Trying not to draw attention to herself, she slowly pulled it out and began texting. The cold Colorado air rushed into her lungs. It gave her a great cover to bundle herself up. She wrapped her wool overcoat and large fuzzy scarf around herself and the phone. As she walked down the stairs, she pressed send and exhaled, praying that Lily would be able to convince people of the corruption that existed and at the very least get her message out.

At the bottom of the stairs stood a row of armed guards, leading the passengers from Air Force One to a waiting, unmarked bus with blacked out windows. Not one of them looked at her in the eyes. She wondered if they possibly mistook her for one of these ruling elite. She suddenly thought back to her eighth grade history class. She heard a quote by Marie Antoinette saying, "Let them eat cake." For the first time ever, she felt what the peasants of France must have endured.

Chapter Sixty-Seven

Lily's phone began making a beeping noise. The sound indicated that she had a new text message. Lily looked at Ben. He was lying down in one of the van's reclining chairs trying to sleep. Many camera men considered the model to be the Lazy Boy of mobile studios. "My friend must be in town." Ben smiled and shook his head, "I'm sorry you won't get to see her."

Her expression changed as she read the text and then listened to the attached message. The more she listened, the larger her eyes grew. When it ended, she pressed a button and handed the phone to Ben, "You've got to hear this." He wasn't sure why he would need to hear a message from someone he had never met. Then, Dani's conversation with Mr. Cash began playing in his ear, Ben was shocked. His worst fears about the last two day's events had just been confirmed. He needed to find Brian and Tiffany and warn them, before it was too late. Lily didn't need to say a word, as she too had just put all the pieces together. She had just landed a front row seat to the story of the century.

Chapter Sixty-Eight

After Sequoia walked away, they sat back down and started to survey the drawing Brian had made of the latest clue. "How did we miss algebra?"

"Look Tiffany, don't beat yourself up over it. I did some student teaching during my under grad, you'd be surprised at how amazing a young person's mind can be." Brian turned and continued to speak as he pointed at the paper, "So, the question is, where's the Point of Origin? And, does this change what we think this artifact is?" Tiffany knew what he was getting at and she had no question in her mind. "I believe he used the phrase, 'Point of Origin' as a double entendre. He was very interested in connections and coincidences."

"OK, but where? Where is the Point of Origin? Maybe a map of the area is a good place to start." Brian jumped up and ran down into the foyer of the small country store. He nearly bumped into a couple walking their Lhasa Apso before he disappeared into the store. Tiffany sat their staring at the numbers and letters that were embedded in the clue. She hadn't taken an algebra class in a long time and didn't quite remember where to start. Brian came bursting out of the door on the opposite side of the store. He looked the other way at first, as if he didn't remember where he had entered. He realized where Tiffany was, and quickly approached the table, "I think I may have figured it out!"

"Well, what?"

"The Four Corners. Look!" He held up the map and pointed at the Four Corners area, where Colorado, New Mexico, Arizona and Utah all meet at one exact point. "Looks like a graph, huh." She smiled and hugged him, "Alright, let's try to figure out what our next step is." Neither of them could hide their excitement. Their faces looked like children on Christmas morning.

Chapter Sixty-Nine

Wes and Rothchild were sitting in his prized silver Mustang, looking right at Brian and Tiffany as they made their discovery. Rothchild could hardly contain her contempt, "Look at these fools, smiling as if they have found the gold at the end of the rainbow." Wes said nothing. He just looked ahead at the targets. Something in his gut felt wrong, what Rothchild just said struck a chord. These Americans, born and bred under the US flag, they were the ones that helped him justify the horrors he committed. A tear welled up in one of his eyes and swelled behind his Ray-Ban sunglasses. Here sat a man who had assassinated leaders and tortured terrorists, all in the name of America. The absolute discipline it took to be him just snapped. Wes couldn't remember the last time he had cried, and yet here he was flowing out of his glasses.

Rothchild was far too self-consumed to even notice. She hadn't taken her eyes off the passenger side, sunshade mirror since they had arrived. Wes opened the door and got out of the car. This apparently awoke the beauty queen from her narcissism, "Where are you going?" Wes kept his back to her, "To the head." He walked right past Brian and Tiffany. *They'll be dead in the next three days.*

Chapter Seventy

Tiffany and Brian both stood up and walked over towards the Jeep. The smell of Juniper inundated the area, and the air was still chilly. Tiffany shivered and Brian instinctively put his arm around her. She leaned her head onto his shoulder and absorbed his body heat. For a brief second, the enormity of the situation seemed to drift away. Slam! A door was slammed a couple of rows over by a tall, blond woman who looked like a runway model. As they approached they Jeep, neither of them wanted to let go. Yet, neither one was sure if the other felt the same way, so they both released. Tiffany looked up at Brian's sky blue eyes and smiled. He smiled back crookedly, giving the appearance of a wink and showing off his boyish dimples. This melted Tiffany's heart and made her knees buckle. She leaned up against the Jeep.

"Hey, you want to drive?" This seemed like a huge step for Brian, who over the past couple of days had seen how controlling Tiffany could be. He appreciated that she was finally able to let someone else take the wheel for awhile. As soon as the engine started, Tiffany's eyes closed, and she felt like the Jeep disappeared. Brian drove out of the parking lot and turned onto the highway heading towards the Four Corners area.

Chapter Seventy-One

Ben put the phone down and looked at Lily, "Do you realize what his means?"

"We're involved in the case of the century." She allowed a little smile to slip out, and Ben returned the favor. "I've always dreamed that I would be able to help solve a big case, but I never could've imagined this."

"I honestly, almost left the station this year to work in real estate. It's pretty well known that I am getting to the age where they replace us with newer, fresher, young women."

"If you don't mind me saying, you don't look a day older than twenty-five."

"At thirty-five, I'll take twenty-five any day." Ben grinned and sat up, taking a more serious tone, "We're about three hours away from the Four Corners area. We need to hit every employee in the area with photos to see if they've seen our guys."

"The photos we have may not be current. They're both from previous yearbooks."

"You'd be surprised at people's ability to make connections between photos and new identities, but that's beside the point. We just want to cover all of our bases."

Chapter Seventy-Two

Dani and a large group of elite socialites were led down a long, winding, stone corridor. The walls were adorned with burning candles and various bas relief of battle scenes from throughout the ages. It was very dark except for the candlelight flickering and bouncing off of the walls, it felt cold and damp. When they came out of the passageway, they entered into a large granite amphitheater. It was massive and foreboding. The rock cavern was filled with artificial light. Dani could see row after row of stone pews all leading down to a small stage in the front. Luxurious tapestries, woven of jewel tone, silk thread and depicting medieval scenes hung on the vast stone walls. Long, flowing theater drapes in red velvet covered the wall behind the stage. A single row of small, wooden chairs were lined up against the blood red backdrop. The setting was macabre and made Dani feel on edge.

Everyone began to take their seats as the lights dimmed and a giant projection screen started to unroll from a slit in the ceiling. A single spotlight came on and illuminated a balcony on the right hand wall that Dani had not noticed, some of the past presidents and major banking moguls sat there. Right under the screen, a monolithic glass podium rose out of the ground. Stepping out of the darkness, President Darius Tobiah entered the room. He was the first African American President in United States history and a beacon of hope for all. He was tall, athletic and compassionate. Dani expected everyone to clap, but nothing happened. He stood there and raised both of his hands, "Court may now begin." Everyone in the room stood up, including Dani. She felt that she may be the only one in the room who had never seen this before.

"Please rise for the Emperor, Mr. Herbert W. Hyde." The crowd erupted with applause. Dani was confused by what was going on. Herbert Sr. walked up onto the podium and grabbed the ivory handled gavel and slammed it down on the sounding block. He began to read off of the virtual teleprompter that appeared in front of him, "Please be seated. Tonight, our resolve shall be tested and if we fail our world empire may not survive its infancy. I know what you're thinking, how can that be, we control everything through the IMF and the Federal Reserve? We have succeeded. We are supreme leaders. Our newest inductee has seen the light that JKF just could not." He paused for a brief applause, "No, this is not a threat from here on Earth, this is something different. Something, that some of you may find out about for the first time tonight. We are not alone in the universe. We have known this for a very long time. Their technology far exceeds our own, so explaining how would be a futile waste of time. Essentially, there are a series of devices that were left with their initial colonies. Four, of the five objects we know about have been secured over time by some of the most powerful men in history. Every great civilization has searched for these relics. You may know them by names such as the Ark of the Covenant or the Holy Grail. All of these have been recovered over time. We, control one of the devices. China, Saudi Arabia and Russia also each possess one. None of us realized that there was a fifth. To our surprise, the device was recently activated, which in turn activated the other four devices spread worldwide. A distress signal was sent out, presumably to the alien creators of these devices. We believe that our filters were able to contain the message within the Earth's atmosphere. However, this was only possible because the fifth object deactivated so quickly. Unfortunately, we lost the artifact and a young couple is now in the process of trying to reactivate the device. Tonight's session, is being called to judge them, and possibly, as a last resort, a call to activate operation Virgin Mary. I understand that this is way ahead of schedule."

Chapter Seventy-Three

After about a half an hour of very strange rituals, the debate began. Dani felt as if she were trapped in a Stanley Kubrick film. The discourse seemed very similar to parliamentary procedure, but crude and lacking in civility. President Tobiah had been cut off at least ten times in the first couple of minutes. Each time, being reminded that he must ask for permission to speak. He was informed that he must also have a second called before he had the right to speak. Not one of these people would stand up for our President. It made Dani sick. Most of the men that did get the opportunity to talk, Dani had never even heard of before. Yet, they were given more respect than any of the elected politicians scattered throughout the room.

A Southern gentleman, dressed in a crisp, white suit spoke in a drawl, "Look y'all, I say we cut these guys down and confiscate the artifact before they can even locate the keys. Where I'm from, people always say, a bird in the hand is better than two in the bush."

Next, a well dressed banker gained the right to speak after the man sat down. The short, gray haired man was so over weight, he appeared to be bulging at the seams. However, in this room he was a rock star. Antonio Verde-Cruz, had ran the Federal Reserve Bank during the thirty year boom that helped cement the transfer, from democracy of the people, to democracy of the corporation, or better known as Free Market Capitalism. He stood up slowly, his deep, puppy dog eyes were set far behind the slick set of dark fifties style glasses. The wrinkles on his face lent to his aura as a wizard, or the man behind the curtain. Dani recognized his raspy voice, and almost felt comfort.

This was an effort on her part to find any semblance of reality in the situation. Her mind raced back to a time when her Father was still alive and used to take her out fishing. He would constantly remind her that if she felt nauseous, she just needed to look for land. He explained how the land can make balance out of the chaos of the sea. Right now, Dani would do anything for some land. However, in this room, she could sadly find none. She was a ship lost at sea. Antonio Verde-Cruz had a familiar tone, but the words shocked her. "We could stop this now, but each of the remaining keys is made of a material, that if weaponized, could destroy our entire planet. This is not my expertise, but should it fall into the wrong hands, it could change the balance of power. As a man of influence, I feel we need to see this all the way through." he stopped and sat down.

The room went silent. Then whisperings between members in the room started to disseminate, as another man rose, "I would like to add to the rebuttal." Again, there were quick seconds by numerous members of the court. Dani noticed that a woman down the row from her was the first to give a second. She found this strange, so she asked Mr. Cash, "Can anyone in the room take time to speak?"

"By being here, you are now a member of the ruling elite. So yes, you can ask for permission. But, I have

157

never seen a first year inductee get a second, and I suggest you just sit there and listen." Dani didn't respond. She watched as the new person, whom she did not recognize talked. He stood tall and handsome his facial structure seemed to be flawless. "I would like to add that our procurement of the precious element also insures no disruption in our current monopoly on the energy market. Can you imagine China with its hands on an energy source that would cut their dependency from our oil conglomerates? The wars in Iraq and Afghanistan would have been for nothing."

Mr. Tobiah jumped up right after the man sat down, "I would like to request time for a rebuttal." Herbert Sr. rolled his eyes, "Any seconds?" Again, the room went silent for the fifteen second waiting period given, for the second call to be made. After fourteen excruciating seconds, Herbert raised the gavel to kill the request. Suddenly, Dani yelled, "Second!" A series of gasps were followed by everyone in the room's eyes falling upon Dani. The look on Mr. Cash's face was one of pure horror. A man with unlimited money and power was brought to his knees by a single word, uttered by his secretary. She sat down and ignored the scathing looks coming at her from every direction.

Mr. Tobiah was clearly surprised, and gave her a nod of thanks, "As it seems I was not meant to speak here today, I will keep this brief. The short sighted views in this room are just another example of why the people will not stand for this. You're saying that in order to save people from knowledge, it would be OK to begin World War III. To top it off, this source of energy could free the people from at least one burden that is holding back our species. Why are you so afraid of freedom?" He sat down and there wasn't a sound in the room, you could have heard a pin drop. With no rebuttal, Herbert Sr. spoke, "I would like to call a recess. Altar boy, call the recess." This was an obvious slap, reminding Tobiah where he stood in the pecking order. He stood back up dejectedly, "The Emperor would like to call a recess for fifteen minutes."

Most people stood up immediately and headed for the restrooms. Dani sat there, trying not to make eye contact with anyone. Mr. Cash leaned over towards her, "You're on your own now." He was a greedy, self serving CEO, who had no idea what right and wrong was, he only knew the desire for power and pleasure.

As he walked off, a hand was placed on Dani's shoulder. She instantly tightened all of her muscles and was scared to look and see who it was. The voice she heard, she couldn't believe. When she turned around, she was face to face with the person who, the public thought was the most powerful man in the world. He stuck out his hand, "Hello. My name is Darius." She smiled, "I'm Dani."

Chapter Seventy-Four

The Captain walked up to Sandy and whispered under his breath, "Can I speak with you in the closet?" They both looked around, trying not to draw attention to themselves. Then they walked briskly down the hall and through the break room, checking around one last time before disappearing into the supply closet. When the door shut, the Captain turned on his flashlight, giving her enough light to see that he was not happy. "What the hell is going on?" Sandy wasn't sure what he was hinting at, "With what?"

"I started to think about what Ben had said. So, I thought I'd go down to St. Anthony's and talk to him about it. But, as you know, he walked out of there today. The surgeon indicated that his injury could be life threatening if it's not properly taken care of, and he walks out. Where the hell is he?" Sandy, already in hot water for punching Lily Levine earlier that day, decided to fess up, "Look Captain, I was just keeping him up to snuff. He was convinced that he may be able to bring them in without any violence."

Right then, the closet door opened, out of the corner of her eye Sandy could see a man wearing a black suit. She sprang forward and planted a huge kiss right on the Captain's lips as the federal agent peered in. He quickly readjusted his perception, and apologized for interrupting, then shut the door and left the two love birds alone. Sandy pulled back, and wiped her lips off with the sleeve from her right arm, "Yuck."

"What do you mean yuck? So anyway, he's headed to the Four Corners area isn't he?" She leaned back against the shelves and sighed, "Yes. And I'm telling you Captain, there's something wrong here, but Ben, he can do this." The Captain almost cracked a smile, "As soon as they cross the state line, the feds will pull out of here and his information flow will stop. So, we need to figure out a way for us to keep him in the loop if they go beyond the border." Sandy smiled and gave him a great big hug, "Sir, I was just wondering if we could keep that kiss just between us. I don't really want people to think I'm..." The Captain interrupted her, "No problem."

Chapter Seventy-Five

Brian and Tiffany were standing directly on top of the Four Corners monument. There wasn't a whole lot there, just a ton of gravel, flat, gray concrete and a few metal medallions embedded in the ground denoting each state. There were flags flying above and you could hear them flapping in the wind, rickety wooden concession stands with faded paint surrounded the entire area. Tiffany was carrying the green backpack which the coveted artifact resided inside of. Brian couldn't help but do the time honored Four Corners stance. He placed two feet in two states and two hands in another two states, effectively placing himself in all four states at once. Wes had brought his son here on their way to an elk hunt a couple of years ago, in between stints in Iraq and Afghanistan. Now, he was sitting there next to a woman that he could not stand, preparing to take out an American couple.

Suddenly, out of the corner of his eye came a vision that made him believe he may be having a flashback. However, what he saw was entirely real. He did in fact see him, and before he could say anything, the sharply dressed man drew his weapon. Wes jumped from the car and engaged the assassin from behind. Rothchild, who in Wes's eyes didn't even deserve to be working with him, had no idea what was going on. Meanwhile, on the other side of the assassin were Brian, Tiffany and the artifact. They were both oblivious to the fact that this man was about to kill them. Wes fired off two shots and the man instantly dropped to the ground dead. The gunfire wasn't even loud enough to startle a horse that was tied up on the other side of the parking lot. Wes always used a silencer.

Tiffany turned around just in time to see the whole event unfold and wasn't sure what to think. "Brian, look." He looked up and saw the same man he had seen earlier at the Mesa Verde general store, bending over a body on the ground. "Is he OK?" Brian asked. Tiffany had already started walking away when Rothchild stepped in front of her brandishing a fire arm. "Not so fast." Brian, stuck in between, wasn't sure what to do. Wes made that pretty simple, "Boy, get over here now." Wes leaned down and grabbed the dead assassin under the arm pits, then looked at Brian, "Grab his legs." Brian wasn't sure who this guy thought he was. "Why should I?" Wes looked up with his piercing green eyes, "Look boy, I just saved your life. So now, you grab his legs." They picked up the body and walked over towards Wes's Mustang. He opened up the trunk and they tossed the body inside. Rothchild brought Tiffany over to the car.

"Well, you really messed this up." Wes bit back, "They'd both be dead if I hadn't acted." Tiffany and Brian just sat there, quietly leaning up against the Mustang, watching Wes and Rothchild argue. Rothchild was still pointing the gun at the two of them, "Now, what are we going to do if we don't get all the pieces? We won't get paid. Who the hell was that anyway?" Wes gave his crooked grin, "His name was Amman, and he was an assassin that I worked with during the first Iraqi war. If I recall, his main employer was the Saudi Arabian government. They must be after the artifact as well."

Rothchild was visibly angry and her tense movements made Brian very nervous, he couldn't take it any longer, "Lady, you're sure drawing a lot of attention to us right now." The entire episode had played out in front of dozens of tourists. Most of them were just trying to get away, but there were a few that stuck around to watch the show. Wes seemed to sense the same thing, "Get in the car and put your gun away." Brian and Tiffany reluctantly got into the back seat, Wes and Rothchild sat in front. He started the car and burned out as they left the parking lot. He turned right onto the highway then looked back at Tiffany, "Is this the right way?" She was not happy, "We're not even sure where we're going. We just figured out that the Four Corners was the Point of Origin, or at least we thought it was"

"What are you talking about?"

"Well, we thought the clue was leading us to a location at the Four Corners monument. But, I'm starting to think that my Dad was talking about it being the Point of Origin for a much larger scale."

"Look, we're going to need to find a new car quick, and you guys need to figure out where we're headed."

"I don't know who the hell you think you are, but I'm not about to do…" Rothchild flung her arm around, slamming the butt of her gun into Tiffany's left temple, instantly knocking her out. When she finally awoke, she could barely make out the sign on a small grocery store. It read, "Frank's Groceries." Brian leaned over and whispered to Tiffany, "Are you OK?" She was still very groggy but was able to respond, "I'll be fine. Where are we?" Rothchild was still in the car. "Shut up back there, before I knock you out again."

The door swung open and Wes bent down inside, "You guys ready?" Rothchild answered, "I'm always ready. Grab your girlfriend handsome." Brian wasn't in any position to argue, so he just leaned down and put Tiffany's arm over his shoulder, "Come on Tiffany. We gotta go."

When they got out, there were two young Indian boys with huge smiles across their faces standing there next to the Mustang. Wes said to them, "Well boys, take care of the body and we'll call it an even trade. Just make sure you keep it covered for a couple of weeks." As soon as Brian and Tiffany emerged from the car, the two boys stopped talking. They jumped into the car and drove it around the back of the store.

"What the hell Wes?" He looked at Rothchild, "You think I wanted to get rid of my baby?" He had a look of deep sorrow on his face that Brian couldn't help but notice. "The answer is no, but here we are. We have the artifact and we have the two that can lead us to the keys. We can't be driving a car that was involved in a murder, especially since all those tourists were just witnesses. Shut up and get in the back. You two, up in the front with me." He turned and pointed at the rusted, old, white Ford F150 pickup, the cab only sat three. Rothchild was not happy, but this was easy money. So, she jumped in the back next to their bags.

Wes waited for Brian and Tiffany to get in then he sat down behind the wheel. He put his left hand around the faded, dark leather steering wheel cover, then reached down, put his right hand on the keys and turned the truck's engine over. He had to put his foot on the gas pedal and pump it a few times before the truck roared to life. It disturbed some birds, which fled the tree branch that was suspended above. He placed it into gear. "Let's hope she holds together for the trip." He then pulled onto the highway. Brian tried to break the tension, "I'm sorry about your car." Wes looked at him and said nothing he just turned back towards the road. Another painful sixty seconds of silence passed. "I'm Wes. Look, we have orders and let's just say, as long as we get all the keys and the artifact back to my employer, we may be able to save your lives."

Tiffany wasn't having any of it she had already come too far and been through too much. Even though she was sitting on the far side of the passenger cab, she violently tried to reach across Brian and hit Wes. Brian held her back. "You think you can kill my Dad and I'm going to help you?" Wes suddenly slammed on his brakes, veering off of the road and coming to a complete stop. "I have never killed any Americans, and I would like to keep that track record going. But you're making that pretty hard right now." Rothchild knocked on the rear sliding window. Wes turned around and opened the window, "What?"

"What? What the hell is going on here? It's bad enough I have to endure…" Wes didn't hesitate. He closed the window, locked it and released the emergency brake, letting the truck give her his response. She bounced around the back of the truck as they fishtailed onto the road again. "Now, where were we?" He yelled over the noise of the truck, "Oh yeah, bottom line, help me or you'll die." Brian tried to make nice, "How do we know we can trust you?"

"Son, you can't trust anyone. But, you can take me by my word. I will do everything in my power to help you make it through this alive." Right then, a black car slammed into the back end of the truck at a very high velocity. Time seemed to stop as the truck swerved around nearly rolling over. Rothchild almost got ejected, but she had latched herself to the dog chains so Wes couldn't jostle her around after the last time. She peered over the side, and down at the small sedan trying to run the truck off of the road. Two men, who appeared to be of Asian descent, were in the car and they were waving weapons in every direction. Rothchild pulled the pistol out of her hip holster and fired off four quick shots. The car flew over the embankment and drove off into the desert. When she turned around Brian and Tiffany were staring right at her. Their eyes were wide open, as were their jaws. Rothchild just sat back down against the cab and closed her eyes ignoring them. Brian and Tiffany both whipped their heads towards Wes, "Why are there so many people trying to kill us over this cube?"

"Cube, huh? Apparently, whatever that artifact, or cube reveals, is dangerous enough for the government to be considering doing the unthinkable, detonating a nuclear weapon in its vicinity in order to hide it." Tiffany's eyes lit up, "Did you say nuclear?"

"Yeah, that was my reaction. If we fail, it will happen. There is no doubt in my mind."

Chapter Seventy-Six

Gavin was Lily Levine's camera man and now cross country chauffer. He was tall, dark and infectiously cute. The epitome of aloha spirit and the laid back Hawaiian lifestyle. He was always helping others by using his sense of humor. Gavin shook her arm, "Did you hear that?" She opened her eyes, "No, I was trying to get some sleep." He pointed at the radio, "There was a report of a shooting at the Four Corners monument." This sprung some life into Lily, who was now checking herself in the mirror. "Well, what time is it? How far away are we?" Gavin looked down for a brief second, grabbed the map and gave it to Lily, "If you open it up and look right at the bottom. Yeah, right there. I think that's where we're at. So, we're about one hour away. You think we'll make it in time to get the story?"

"Well, we'd better, or this may be my last hurrah." Gavin didn't like that idea, because it meant he may lose his job. "We'll get there. Pele is with us tonight." Suddenly, Gavin began to make a deep rumbling sound and started to chant;

The Point of Origin

"Ai Noho ana Ke Akua.
Ke aloha ai no ho ana ke akua i ka na hele hele.
I alai i'a e teti ohu ohu e ka ua koko.
E na kino malu i ta lani.
Malu e hoe.
E ho'o ulu mai, ana o Laka i kona kahu 'owau 'owau noa.
Ua i kea."

His voice went up with a trill at the end of each sentence and the sound was almost hypnotic. Lily had never even heard Gavin talk about his Hawaiian heritage before. She was slightly taken aback by his performance. However, somehow she felt calmed by the soothing vibration of his voice. At this point she was willing to let any god give her a hand.

Chapter Seventy-Seven

Brian looked at Tiffany then at Wes, "We think we know where the first key might be. But it could be a dead end if we misinterpreted the clues left by her Dad." Wes grinned, "OK, so where to?" Tiffany pulled a map out of her sweatshirt pocket. "Tes Nez Iah." she pointed to a tiny dot on the map. Wes had never heard of it, not many people had. However, for some reason Tiffany's Father was leading them there, to a place that is so small, it isn't even designated as an actual town. "What are we looking for?"

"We're looking for a bridge."

Chapter Seventy-Eight

The hallway that Dani was walking down had a dark and dreary feel that gave her the chills. Even that could not squash her excitement. Here she was, walking next to the President of the United States, and he wanted to talk to her. "Here we are." He opened the door and motioned for her to step in. Apparently, the President was not afforded a luxury suite, rather a janitor's office. He sat down, behind the janitor's desk. Dani sat on a cold steel, folding chair across from the President. "Well Dani, as you can see things aren't really what they seem to be in the good ol' US." His face was filled with regret and sadness. "I've learned a great deal Mr. President."

He leaned forward in his seat, "Dani, you may be the key to saving this country. In that room, there are good people that have been misled. I would go as far as to say, brainwashed to be distrustful and fearful of the people." Dani smiled, it delighted her to know that he was not one of them, for the first time it gave her hope. Darius had seen this many times in his life, as he had always been good at reading people's emotions and taking advantage of it.

"Now, if I can only give the people in that room that aren't too far gone, the same feeling you just had, then we may be able to give that couple out there enough time to expose the truth and set us all free." Dani's eyes swelled up with tears. It was as if she had just been spoken to by Martin Luther King Jr. or Mahatma Gandhi. "If you second me, and give me a chance to talk, the chicken hawks won't be able to do or say anything about it."

Dani's face drastically changed, all of her color drained and the hope transformed to fear, "Mr. Gildman-Cash said they would kill me for speaking." The President's face softened and he reached out one of his large hands, "And yet you spoke already. Dani, my family is in grave danger and will most likely be killed because of my words here tonight." He paused and tried desperately to hold back his emotions, "But this, this is our chance to make a difference. Not just for our country, but for the world."

Dani's face slowly changed back to one of hope and her eyes lit up, "We don't really have any other choice do we?" He smiled and squeezed her hand, "You always have a choice, and I'll leave it up to you. But, just to be safe there are going to be a couple of my private security guards with you the rest of the night. I understand if you decide not to help, but I hope you'll think about it." He stood up and gently let go of her hand, "Time to head back. I'll trust you'll make the right decision. And again, thank you."

Chapter Seventy-Nine

Wes pulled off the two lane highway just before the bridge at Tes Nez Iah. They were in the middle of the desert and it was desolate to say the least, just random dilapidated mobile homes, various cactus, Yuccas and dirt. Brian couldn't help but comment, "This is it? Not much here." Wes looked at Brian, "Not sure we're here for site seeing." The old truck rolled to a stop just before the bridge. "Here's a bridge, and this is Tes Nez Iah, now what?" Tiffany answered with disdain in her voice, "That's all we have to go on."

"What? How is it that they're living out here with no..." Tiffany didn't wait to hear what he was saying. She jumped out of the truck and headed for the bridge. Rothchild unbuckled the dog chains from her belt and jumped out of the truck, following closely behind Tiffany. Brian looked at Wes, and shrugged his shoulders, "Women." Then he slid over, hopped out and followed the two females, down towards the bridge. Wes straggled behind.

When Wes finally turned the corner under the bridge, he was stunned to find Tiffany sitting down next to an elderly Indian man. He wore modern denim jeans, but had long black braids that were peppered with gray, several turquoise necklaces layered around his neck, an intricately beaded vest and an eagle feather in his hair. Tiffany was trying to get Rothchild to put down her gun. Brian stepped forward, out of the way when he heard Wes's voice from behind, "Rothchild put your gun away. We're not here to hurt anyone, just to find something." The old man held up his hand, "Please be seated." Brian and Wes sat down next to the small, burning fire, opposite of the others. Rothchild was not thrilled and was trying to find a smooth place to sit.

"I am Red Feather. Some call me Túhikya or Medicine Man. I have been waiting for you for some time now, nearly two weeks. Luckily, my home is right down the gully. But these old clothes are starting to grow a little foul." Tiffany smiled, "Why have you been waiting?"

"Your Father gave me something, and asked that I share its importance with you before you complete your destiny and free my people." Tiffany wasn't sure what he was talking about, but clearly this was where they were supposed to be.

Chapter Eighty

Back at the station, the feds had just informed Captain Barba that he was being cut out of the loop and that they were moving to Albuquerque, New Mexico, to be closer to the suspects. Captain Barba slammed his clipboard down on his desk. Meanwhile, a man wearing a dark suit confiscated his files and left him standing there with nothing left to help his guy, the one that was out there risking his neck. Just then, Sandy came into the office, "Sir, you seem really upset, but we're running out of time. I put one of those radio microphones on donkey number one as they were leaving. As long as we're within three miles, we can keep audio surveillance on them. Here's your jacket, come on."

"What about the station, and a warrant? We can't..." She cut him off as she was pulling him towards the exit, "You and I both know that sometimes you have to break protocol to do the right thing." He surveyed around the station and everyone looked as if they had just seen a car wreck. He shook himself loose and yelled, "Get back to work and hold down the fort!" He looked at Sandy and they both walked out of the station.

Chapter Eighty-One

"Koyaanisqatsi, life out of balance." Red Feather placed a small pinch of tobacco into the pipe. First, he turned to the south and called upon fire with his prayers, then he made a quarter turn to the west and called to the wind with his prayers. Again, he made a turn to the north and his prayers were directed at stone. Once more he made a quarter turn clockwise, towards the east. This time he prayed to the water. Finally, he made one last turn back into his original position and called to his Mother, his Father and his Self with all of his hopes and prayers. He lit the tobacco, took a puff and then he spoke as he passed around the sacred pipe, "You must first ask for forgiveness, then inhale. As you exhale, list the atrocities you, yourself have done to our Mother Earth. Then, and only then, can I tell you of our truth, one that guides us and gives us hope."

Each person in the group silently went through the ritual, blowing smoke into the fire causing an array of amazing visions swirling in the air. The old man hummed and played a small drum, transforming the landscape into something absolutely incredible. Tiffany passed the pipe and blew out a huge plume of smoke. It first, took the shape of an eagle, but then dispersed to look like an angel. Red Feather knew Tiffany had seen it. "Star People." No one in the circle seemed to notice, but Tiffany's mind was racing. *This man knows what we're about to find.*

Just then, the Red Feather received the pipe from Rothchild. The old man looked up and down all four of them from head to toe, "Koyaanisqatsi, life out of balance. My Father told me and my brother of a vision he once had. He believed that one day, one of us would help a young woman call back our great White Brother to fulfill the Hopi prophecy." He took a puff from his pipe and passed it to Tiffany, "When my brother and your Father contacted me, I knew that the time had finally come. The prophecy is one of great promise or great destruction. If, you can somehow call the Great Blue Star, it will save us from ourselves and we will enter the fifth world whole. There has been no time since the great lizards that our Mother has been so out of balance. The Hopi have held true, and await the day of fulfillment. I have to admit that I didn't always believe that this would come to be, but when your Father and my brother showed me the artifact, my doubts were put to rest." Brian reached down between his legs and pulled the cube out of the backpack, "This artifact?"

"Son, you should be careful with how you handle that thing. Everyone I know, who has touched it has died." He handed a small leather pouch to Tiffany. When she reached inside she found a diamond shaped stone and a piece of paper that was rolled up and tied with a string. "Place this on the artifact, and you'll see what I'm speaking of." Tiffany looked at Brian. Her excitement was boiling over as her chest rose with every deep breath she took, "Can you place it on the ground?" Brian looked over at Rothchild, then at Wes. Wes nodded, "Sounds interesting."

Brian put the artifact on the ground and Tiffany placed the second of five keys into position. Suddenly, it sprang to life like a computer, the strange hieroglyphs on the cube started to glow a florescent blue color. A beam of light shot out of the top, hovering above it was the head of an old man resembling an Indian, with long hair and a full, white beard. "Hello." it spoke in Hopi. Tiffany and Brian asked at the same time, "What did he say?" The head turned to them, "English, I love English."

Chapter Eighty-Two

After the customary introductions and strange, pagan rituals, a number of men stood and began tossing the fate of the Southwest around the chamber. Dani was in a daze, not hearing a word that any one of them said. She just sat there, staring through the sea of heads at Mr. Tobiah. Her hands were sweaty. She rubbed them together then tried to take a deep breath to calm herself down. Right then, Mr. Tobiah stood up and asked to speak. The Emperor hit the gavel and asked for a second to the President's request. Dani stood, as if she had just been called on in class, "Second." When she sat back down, she could feel the eyes staring at her again. She just kept looking at Darius and blocked out everything else as he began to speak.

"Today, I have heard you relay the fact that we have no idea what the artifact will actually do. We have also speculated that if the information was made public, our current religions would crumble and our society would collapse. If I have learned anything about Americans, it's that they will cling on to what they know, even in the face of irrefutable evidence. It would take months even years for us to…" Mr. Hyde Sr. interrupted, "The point Sir?" Mr. Tobiah scowled at the Emperor, "My point Sir, is that we sit here, deliberating how to suppress knowledge from the people. Should we kill a couple of innocent people, should we detonate a nuclear device near the Grand Canyon where the Colorado River runs through? Have any of you thought about the impact that will have on Southern California? We're risking the lives of millions to hide the truth from the people. Does that make any sense? I move that we add another option, to allow the activation and deal with the truth." Mr. Tobiah turned, and peered through the crowd catching the eye of Dani. He walked over and sat at his seat just behind the podium. Dani, sounding very unsure rose and said, "Second." Hyde Sr. hit the gavel and spoke with anger in his voice, "Votes will be counted when the last of you has placed your ballot, after the two hour lobby period has expired." He hit the gavel again.

The entire room became frenzied over the recent development. Dani just sat there watching as the people conversed about the vote. Mr. Tobiah made his way through the crowd, shaking hands and pleading with them to vote for the option. He slowly got closer, and smiled at Dani every chance he could to try and reassure her that he was trying to make it over to her. Apparently, he wasn't moving fast enough, because Dani stood up, and walked over to him, "Excuse me Sir." Mr. Tobiah looked up at her. The onlookers were all preying upon them like feasting vultures on a dead horse. Mr. Tobiah leaned in towards Dani and whispered, "Thank you. We bought them at least two more hours to find the keys." Dani smiled and Mr. Tobiah walked her back towards her chair.

Chapter Eighty-Three

Tiffany's jaw dropped, as Brian introduced himself to the cube, "Hello. My name is Brian." The hologram was floating there in front of them. At first, it appeared as the head of an older Indian. However, as it spoke to Brian the image began to look more Anglo Saxon in origin. It moved around the circle, and introduced itself to each member of the group, each time it morphed into a figure that represented the individuals own heritage. In front of Rothchild it was Norse, for Wes and Red Feather, it returned to the original Native American Indian figure. Then, it got back around to Tiffany. "That's strange." Tiffany's big brown eyes looked up at the image, "You think I'm strange? You're a talking box."

"It's not you that's strange. Your ancestry contains all four of the original DNA strands we planted. Very rare." Brian could see she was starting to get frustrated and he wanted to get to the point. Who knew how long this cube could power itself. "Excuse me, Sir." The head flew back towards him, morphing into an Anglo Saxon figure once more, with white hair and a long beard. "What are you?" he asked. The cube replied, "I'm a Global Origination Device. The Wotomi people, of the planet Pota were the first of your Fathers. They ruled over a society that worshiped science. Their great civilization had run its course, and the planet rejected its people, in something similar to what you know as an apocalypse. But the people were industrious and devised a plan to save themselves. They boldly found at least two other planets in their own universe that could sustain them, they needed only minor genetic modifications to make this possible."

At this point, graphs, charts and three dimensional models of the original DNA strands were all projected out of the cube. Tiffany and Brian were blown away. Tiffany got up and walked over to the hologram of the DNA, "Oh my God." Tears started to flow from her eyes uncontrollably. She wasn't sad or angry. These tears were tears of joy. Wes spoke to Brian, "What's wrong with her?" Tiffany looked at Wes scornfully, "You may not understand what this cube just said, but do you see this DNA strand right here?"

"Yes."

"This is the missing link. The link that nobody ever imagined, would lead us to this. Don't you get it? We are so much more than anyone ever thought. This will change everything. The human perception will have to reevaluate everything that they know." Wes was still looking at her blankly, so Brian explained it to him in simple language to help him out. "What she means is, that this strand right there proves that we do indeed have some relation to apes. It's also possible that what our religions have taught us isn't exactly true."

The cube interrupted, "Actually, your religions are based on programming in various genes of your DNA. This was in order to try and avoid past mistakes. They tried to start colonies here many times, but they had problems with the first couple of DNA strands. In the Tokpela, first world, our strains gave us major problems. Although each planet could support life, they all needed certain adaptations. So, we had to cross-clone with an indigenous species. The species that we split with, in the first world wasn't evolved enough, and they destroyed themselves quickly. Tokpa and Kuskurza, the second and third worlds, suffered a similar fate. The fourth world, Túwaqachi, has worked out so far. All told, it takes nine worlds on each planet before we exhaust all life. Currently, we are in the fourth world on the planet you call Earth. During the third world, there was a species of Neanderthal that we thought was perfect. Four different races or strains were created, all with the same molecular DNA. They became the first human beings. We worked alongside each other, building massive structures to help balance the planet. As the populations grew a curious thing happened, the four races began to clash. We tried, but ultimately they used our knowledge of power to destroy themselves. The continent that they resided on sunk to the depths of the ocean. We saved some very young children and sent them to the four corners of the Earth. We tried a hand's off experiment, and your world quickly became unique. For the first time, an entire world would be given to the clones to let them progress on their own. As a result, most of the population has grown too large for the planet. There is a lack of balance, both physically and mentally, and despite all the onlookers and their hope, this world may end in disaster. The signs from the first three failed world's are there. Warring strains have decimated, and in some cases been entirely exterminated. The others and soon themselves..."

Tiffany interrupted, "How could you possibly know any of this? Can you read our minds or the future?" The cube's head shifted and looked at her. It morphed into a head that she could not place, the others couldn't either. The elongated skull had the appearance of a cone and the chin seemed much longer and more pronounced than any human's. The face looked to be female, and yet almost male. "This is what the original people looked like. You, my dear, are the closest thing on this planet. You are one of us." It shot out two new DNA strands, "The one on the left belongs to the original species placed on this planet, the one on the right, that's yours. Take out the Neanderthal gene and you would be complete."

"I feel like I'm complete just the way I am."

"Be that as it may, I was the fourth implant in the middle of the final continent. I have had many keepers. I cannot read minds or the future. Time as you know it, is not in my programming. What my programming does have is a way to give me all possible scenarios based on the past three world's experiences. Certain triggers are given to us, and you my dear, are a trigger. Complete the keys and you'll find out what to." The cube shut off. Tiffany and Brian both looked at Red Feather and said in unison, "What happened?"

"It told you what it had to say."

"But..." He laughed, "You'll have to change some of what you believe."

Chapter Eighty-Four

The 9 News van pulled into the Four Corners parking lot and stopped adjacent to a tribal police barricade. Ben started to get up, but Lily put her hands out, "Sit and relax. These Indian cops don't have the same attitude about me, they don't see my show." Ben laughed, "So, you think they'll tell you more than me, a fellow officer? Here's an idea. You interview the partner, while I talk to the main man, then we switch." Lily looked down at Ben and pointed to his bandages, "What about your shoulder?"

"I feel fine, now let's hit it." They jumped out of the van and walked over to the yellow caution tape surrounding an empty crime scene. Gavin followed close behind, with the camera running, catching the entire episode on tape. Ben reached down and pulled out his badge, as Lily simultaneously held up her microphone. Ben split to the left and went towards the older officer, Lily headed to the right. Ben introduced himself and told the man a story about the search for a Bonnie and Clyde type couple. The officer lit up and told Ben that the onlookers did see his couple. However, it had been a second couple that had killed the man and taken Ben's twosome as hostages. Meanwhile, Lily was getting the exact same answer and neither of them actually knew where the growing group of suspects was headed.

"Maybe towards the south is the only indication we have." the officer told Lily. Having very little time, they both thanked the person they were interviewing and walked back to the van. Gavin was surprised, "That's it, we're done?" Lily turned to him, "We've got to get after them now." They all jumped into the van and took their seats. Lily brought Gavin up to speed, "The couple that has them hostage will kill them, and if that happens the story's over." Gavin gave her a funny look, "And two innocent people will be dead." She hit him in the shoulder, "Yes, but I don't want to think about it that way."

"Why not?" Gavin questioned. Ben popped into the conversation as they exited the parking lot, giving the answer, "Because we're going to have to save them from two trained assassins, and that's not an easy thing to deal with." Gavin almost drove off the road. Then he turned back to look at Ben, "You mean we're gonna..." Ben pointed and yelled, "Watch what you're doing!" Gavin corrected the vehicle and looked ahead at the road. Ben started talking before Gavin could say anything else. "You two can stay out of the way and I'll do the work. Just make sure you get it on tape. I don't want them saying I committed suicide or some damn thing."

Chapter Eighty-Five

Rothchild reached over and tapped Wes on the knee. She tilted her head to the side, signaling that she wanted him to come with her. He looked at Red Feather, "Would it be OK if I went with Rothchild? I think she needs to use the restroom." The old man nodded in approval as he continued to hum and drum. Tiffany and Brian watched in anticipation as they walked away. Brian turned to Tiffany and whispered, "Give me your phone." Tiffany handed him the phone and whispered back, "Who can you call?" Brian held up a business card, the one Tiffany had gotten from Officer Lovato. Brian knew if he texted Ben, it wouldn't be long before cops figured out a way to track the phone. Then maybe they would be saved from whoever was after them. He entered a text into the phone. *"Tes Nez Iah. Help! B+T"* he hit send and put the phone back in his pocket.

Meanwhile, behind the truck Rothchild was squatting down with her pants around her knees, relieving herself. "Jesus, Rothchild everyone on the road can see you." Rothchild finished and pulled her underwear and pants over her exposed buttocks. "Listen, you know we have to kill them. Why not do it now? We could take that cube and sell it on the black market. We would get way more money then we're owed now, and no nuke, win, win."

"Look, we need all of it, and now that we know what this artifact holds, I'm sure our bosses will see fit to us getting what we deserve." Rothchild rolled her eyes, "How, you plan on black mailing them?"

"I know that it's worth more with all the pieces. And I know that those two will find it way faster than we will."

"What about these other assassins?"

"We have to assume that more will be coming. I don't think they'll give up easily. So, we need..." Rothchild interrupted and stepped in close to his chest, "We need to just kill them and leave." Filled with anger, Wes pushed her back and yelled, "This is my country, and I will not abandon it!" A tear fell from his eye and his fists clinched. Wisely, Rothchild grinned, "OK Wes, you're right." He stood there until she turned and walked back to the Indian's fire. He knew that if he turned his back on her, he'd be dead.

Chapter Eighty-Six

Ben's phone beeped and he looked at the text message from a number that he had never seen. He looked at the screen and read the message, *"Tes Nez Iah. Help! B+T."* He couldn't believe it. They had remembered the card Ben had given to Tiffany. He turned to Lily, "Got that map?" She looked at Ben and handed him the map, "Good news?"

"Not sure, but...aah ha. There it is. I think we're about thirty minutes away." Lily couldn't contain her excitement, "How could you know?"

"It must be my irresistible charm, because they just sent me this text." He handed her the phone. She looked at the message, then handed the phone to Gavin and yelled, "Alright then, we're in business!" She pumped her fists in the air, "So, what's the plan?" Ben stopped, "We don't want to get too worked up. We're not sure if they'll even be there by the time we get there. It would probably be smart to make contact on a more casual level. We should survey the situation first."

Lily wasn't sure what to say or do. She looked out the window in thought. Ben asked for his phone back. Gavin handed it to him. He went through the contact list until he came to Captain Barba's number. He hit send and began talking to the Captain. After Ben finished explaining what had happened, the Captain replied, "We're trying to run surveillance on the feds, but they checked into the Holiday Inn, and haven't said anything about the case." He decided that by going back to the station, and calling in a couple of favors, they might be able to help. They just needed to triangulate Brian's cell phone.

Chapter Eighty-Seven

Wes and Rothchild came walking around the corner to find Brian and Tiffany packing up their things. They were helping the Túhikya put out his fire. Brian shoveled dirt with an old box from a twelve pack of Coke. Tiffany leaned down and helped Red Feather up off the ground. He dropped the drum and nearly fell over as he tried to reach for it. Tiffany, instinctively shot out her leg and caught it cradled on her foot. She lifted it up, and the old man smiled warmly, "White Brother." Tiffany didn't quite understand, because he spoke in Hopi. She assumed he had said, "Thank You", so she replied, "You're welcome." He shook his head and chuckled as he walked slowly towards Wes. Brian finished putting out the fire and spoke softly to Tiffany, "Are you sure we should take him? It's going to be pretty dangerous."

"Look, we need to make sure we find the next key. When we get all five pieces together, then his knowledge may come in handy." Brian wasn't sure, as far as he could see this old man was still clinging on to a dying culture, devoid of science. Tiffany however, was functioning on an entirely different level, able to understand things that Brian wasn't ready to experience. She had read about how the distinction between a genius and others was the ability to control intellectual creativity. A genius has the ability to control their thoughts, and in many instances their reality. She could sense when she was in the presence of another who could also function at this same level. Walking ever so painstakingly towards Wes, there was an old man whose wisdom far exceeded that of most people. She stared in total awe.

Brian felt a tinge of jealousy for a brief second. Then, he jolted back to reality and remembered that they were not a couple, he had no right to feel that emotion. Tiffany could see Brian was in need of her attention. She looked at him, and put her hand on his shoulder. Brian instantly felt better. The Túhikya hobbled right past Rothchild and straight up to Wes. He put his hand on Wes's forehead, "Lost, koyaanisqatsi."

"Yes. I know the world is out of balance." The old man shook his head, "No. You, you are out of balance. Don't lose you." He took his hand off of Wes and continued walking past him. Rothchild asked, "What the hell was that about?" Wes, annoyed as ever with her attitude, bit his tongue and quietly answered her, "He's just an old man." Rothchild rolled her eyes and walked back towards the truck, hitting Wes in his arm with her shoulder, as she walked by. Wes ignored her yet again, and asked Brian and Tiffany, "I take it we need the old man to come with, huh?" Tiffany took her hand off of Brian's shoulder, and replied, "Looks like you'll have to ride in back like a dog." Wes looked at Brian. His face expressed his complete frustration with the two women he was stuck with on this mission. He could have said no, he could have stayed in retirement, but no. He left his fiancé and son waiting at home in Wyoming. To top it off, here he was, being belittled by one woman and threatened by another.

Suddenly, a shot rang out. It sounded infinite in the vast openness of the Southwestern mesa. "Another assassin!" Rothchild yelled as she spun in slow motion with her two pistols blazing. By the time Wes had a chance to get his gun out, and reach a viable area for retaliation, Rothchild had already been hit. There were two assassins, dressed in all black, with hoods and dark sunglasses. The Túhikya was able to take cover behind the truck, while Brian and Tiffany were perched down in back of Wes, still under the bridge. Another shot rang out. It hit the dirt about two inches from Wes's left foot. All three of them slid down lower to avoid the next shot. Tiffany asked with concern, "Where's Red Feather?" Wes looked up and saw Rothchild slowly crawling across the desert, towards the Túhikya. Behind, she left a trail of blood causing the dirt to clump together in tiny, red beads. Wes turned to Brian and Tiffany, "He's OK, but Rothchild's been hit." The gleaming smile on his face, when he said that she had been hit, was one of joy and excitement.

Brian recognized the look, it was the same look his mother had when his Father had finally drunk himself to death. This made Brian think his hunch about Wes was right. He may be able to be trusted. Tiffany asked, "Where's the fire coming from?" Wes pointed back up towards the road, over his left shoulder. "How many?" Wes held up one finger, but then shook his head and held up two, "Two still shooting." Two shots from the same area hit the dirt. Wes returned fire to hold them in their current positions.

The standoff was suddenly interrupted by a flying news van. It came sliding to a stop in between the assassins and the bridge, nearly tipping over in the process. The occupants of the van apparently had no idea what they had just stumbled into Wes thought. To his surprise, a man burst out of the side door firing at the assassins, hitting one as he ran to join the other three on the embankment. He slid in, like it was home plate, forgetting about the bullet wound to his shoulder. He laid there on the ground for a second in agonizing pain, before catching his breath, "Hi there." Wes answered, "Thanks for the help." Ben looked at Brian and Tiffany, "Are you OK?"

Chapter Eighty-Eight

Captain Barba and Sandy walked into the station at a frantic pace, then immediately headed in separate directions. They had called ahead and already had a trace on the phone, giving Ben and Lily a chance to find and help the two suspects from Golden, Colorado. When they realized how close they were, they came up with a plan to drop Lily and Gavin off a quarter of a mile down the road, so that they wouldn't be in harm's way. Ben was going to drive the van in, survey the situation, then take action.

It worked to perfection, and now Sandy and the Captain were preparing to put together a team to help Ben save Brian and Tiffany. Sandy knew full well that she would probably lose her badge for this. It did not matter. She would choose the right thing before she sold out to a broken system. She knew police officers who held grudges against people, and would do everything they could to destroy their lives. Sandy, Ben and the Captain, were of a different breed, their loyalty to principle and honesty could not be bought. Sadly, in America today, Sandy knew that all too often, money was king, leaving even the proudest of people to sell out.

She reached the server room and entered to find Officer Nakamoto glued to his state of the art Promethean board. These multimedia boards allow a very interactive experience with the computer, mimicking the movements of your hand. He was staring at two dots blinking near the Four Corners area, one red and one blue. He reached up his hand, putting his fingers on the board. He brought his index finger and thumb slowly together triggering a function that allowed the image to zoom all the way into Tes Nez Iah. "This is live satellite footage." Nakamoto told Sandy with pride. She could see the news van parked behind the old truck. The two blinking lights were visible, but the resolution was not the best. "Can you clear it up?"

"Yeah." he turned his hand clockwise and the picture suddenly went into focus. There were two people lying on the dirt in front of the truck and one crouched down behind. It appeared that the two blinking dots were under a bridge and seemed to be taking fire. "How long has it been going on?" Then, she saw another small figure heading towards the back of the bridge. Sandy immediately called Ben. He answered, "Kind of in the middle of ..." Sandy cut him off, "Listen, and don't ask how I know. There's someone coming at the back of the bridge right now!"

Chapter Eighty-Nine

Ben hung up the phone. "We got company coming back there. I'll…" Wes held up his hand as he sprung into action. He effortlessly leaped over Tiffany and Brian. "Hold 'em off with a couple of shots. I'll take out this side and end this." He ran quietly to the far side of the bridge where he met the assassin just as he came around the corner. Grabbing the barrel of the gun, he used the momentum to spin the assassin's body around. His arm quickly sliced down and a knife penetrated the upper leg of the assassin. At the same time, he snapped the assailant's arm causing him to drop his weapon. Next, Wes dropped down and did a leg sweep, sending the assassin flat onto his back. Simultaneously, he lifted his arm and jabbed his knife into the chest of the attacker. He didn't hesitate. He pulled out the knife, jumped up and moved quickly up the other side of the bridge. Out of the corner of his eye he caught Lily and Gavin videotaping the whole thing. As he rounded the final corner, he was already firing his weapon, hitting the last of the assassins, and dropping him dead.

When he came back around to make sure everyone was OK he yelled, "Coast is clear!" No one came out of their hiding places until after they actually saw Wes. Rothchild never stood up. Red Feather announced, "The cold one is gone." Then he stood up, ready and smiling before stepping over her dead body. Ben held up his gun at Wes, and told him, "Freeze." Wes gave him a crooked grin and the Túhikya intervened. Tiffany and Brian looked at each other in confusion. They didn't understand why the old man wanted to keep Wes around. He didn't give any reason why.

"Every person here is of vital importance to what we need to do." Ben looked at the old man quizzically. "Haven't you already taken a leap of faith to be here?" Ben nodded reluctantly. "I thought so." The Túhikya spoke as he put his hand on the barrel of Ben's gun, lowering it. Lily and Gavin were peering off of the bridge at the scene below. The old man's attention quickly changed focus and he yelled, "And you two up there, shut that camera off!" Lily and Gavin stood up and hurriedly started walking away, down the road. Brian turned to Tiffany, "Isn't that..." She cut him off, "Lily Levine." The disgust in her voice was not hard to pick up on. Brian's feeling was mutual.

Red Feather turned to Wes, "Pure heart, now where are we headed?" Wes gave a questioning look, but went along, "Not my call chief. Ask Professor X over there." The old man looked at Brian and Tiffany, "Which one of you is Professor X?" Tiffany stepped forward, "I believe the Neanderthal is referring to me." The old man shook his head in sorrow, "You lower yourself below those you disdain when you use a condescending tone." She accepted his criticism, then reached into her pocket and grabbed out the rolled up paper he had given her earlier. She quickly untied the string and opened it up;

The Point of Origin

Clue #5
AD -8/3x – 54 (0, 54)

PAKWT

***

Brian and Tiffany went on to explain that they needed to head to the next location on the map. "Based on the algebra equation and the coordinate graph, the 'Y' axis determines that Window Rock is the next destination." Red Feather smiled knowingly, "Your Father must have really had a deep understanding of the Puebloan Indian culture." Tiffany's mind was racing with possibilities for how this all made sense. "I can see Window Rock and Mesa Verde, but why Tes Nez Iah?" He laughed when Tiffany asked him, "Because this is my home."

The growing band of travelers decided to leave the old truck behind and ride together in the mobile studio for the remainder of the journey. Wes went to go retrieve his bag from the truck bed before they continued on to Window Rock. The Túhikya quietly stepped up behind Wes as he grabbed the suitcase filled with weapons. He gently placed his hand on top of Wes's and lowered it, "We will not need anything in there where we are going." He reluctantly left his small arsenal behind and got into the van with the others.

Chapter Ninety

Sandy ran down the hall past a few empty cubicles. The wind she created blew papers off the top of one of the file cabinets. She reached Captain Barba's office and blurted out, "Sir!" as she entered the office. He held up his hand because he was on the phone. Sandy couldn't imagine who was so important. The Captain knew what was at stake here. Then, she overheard him say, "Goodbye Mr. Vice President." He turned to look at Sandy and his head dropped. The look on his face made Sandy think that what he had been told was very bad. "What? What is it?"

"That was the Vice President. He wants me to report directly to him regarding Agents Pope and Swanson. I don't know, I think we may have gotten ourselves in over our heads."

"Snap out of it. Now get out of your seat, and let's be Ben's eyes and ears."

"Thanks Sandy." He took a deep breath and pulled himself together, "OK. Ben has made contact. The entire group is headed to the next location." Captain Barba did not turn around. The tone in his voice was familiar to Sandy, that of disgust. In that moment, she knew he was still up to the task that he bared. "Next location?" she asked, "He should apprehend them and bring them home. What the hell is this next location?"

"I talked to Ben and he made contact with the suspects. He gave me the impression that there wasn't much of a choice. He did text us two photos. But crap, if he doesn't arrest them, he's putting us all in a position of liability. We'll all be charged with aiding and abetting. We'll lose our badges. Is that what you want?" Sandy rolled her eyes, she was steadfast, "Sir, we've already crossed that line today. Why not see it through?"

Captain Barba took another deep breath, then made a fist and pumped it in front of himself. "Live with passion." He stood up tall and smiled. Sandy had seen him do this many times to change his state of mind. She used to think that it was hocus pocus, but had found herself, trying to use it sometimes. The Captain walked towards the door, he looked at Sandy, "Let's help our man." He walked past Sandy and out of the room. Sandy quickly followed.

Chapter Ninety-One

Half way to Window Rock, the old man broke the silence, "I'm not sure what you guys have planned, but the sun is going to be down by the time we get to Window Rock." Tiffany and Lily were riding in the rear of the news van with him, along with Wes and Ben. Gavin and Brian sat in the front. Tiffany was quick to remind the group that they couldn't afford to stay in any one spot for long. Wes agreed with her, "You see this tracking device?" He took out a small, round device that looked like part of an IPod. "It has a fixed position on the artifact that Brian has up there between his legs." Tiffany sighed, "That explains why these assassins seem to know where we're at."

Wes grinned and elaborated, "The people that hired me are at the top and none of us will ever be safe again." Ben interrupted, "I'm a police officer and I can tell you, that even the feds are involved, FBI, CIA, Homeland Security, you name it." Lily added, "My friend, who alerted us to your location was transported to Cheyenne Mountain on Air Force One. Who knows what level this stops at?" Wes and Ben both fought to get out the same question, "So why's the cube so important?"

Tiffany looked at Lily, Ben, Wes and finally the old man. She knew that even if she explained the entire thing, they still wouldn't understand. Red Feather saw her frustration and helped her with an eloquently simple explanation. "Her Father was studying some unique phenomenon near and around the Four Corners area. He wanted to use it as a source of power. The kind of power you see the country going to war for. I can' t pretend to understand what it was, but he and my brother stumbled upon a cave filled with life size Kachina dolls surrounding the artifact. It was quite an impressive sight, at first glance it almost looked like an old movie set. My brother immediately knew it had to do with our prophecy of the Pahána, the White Brother who will return to save our people. Her Father, the Professor, was a scientist and had very little understanding of what this all meant. He looked to my brother for all things Hopi, and it seems he was a great student. Her Father rescued the artifact and in the process, witnessed my brother's execution. He did not feel right about things and had come back to check on the artifact, my brother had stayed behind to archive the findings in the cave. Apparently, when the artifact is moved, it gives off a signal that can be tracked. Within three days, your Father was dead. And now..."

Ben interrupted, "But that doesn't explain why the government, and who knows who else is after that cube, and want to have it so badly, that they're willing to kill for it." Red Feather grinned, "I was getting there. Not that the money from the energy source isn't enough motive. As Tiffany can tell you, the information the artifact contains will change what modern civilization considers their most important philosophies and moral standings. This is a very scary thought for those in the upper echelon, because they use those very ideas in order to control the people. They are literally willing to do anything to keep the information suppressed." Lily, in reporter mode asked, "Suppress what information?" He took a deep breath, "We have been trying to tell you for centuries. Many elders have made trips to the United Nations, and the US Congress, among other places to warn them. Each time, the warnings were not heard. Our government has done exactly what we warned against."

Ben was more than a little frustrated. "So, you warned them and now they're carrying out their version of operation clean up?" Wes broke in, "It's so much more than that. That cube up there is alien. I mean little green monster, out of this world, alien." Ben and Lily looked at each other then looked back at Tiffany and the old man, as if looking for confirmation that this was true. Tiffany answered, "Not only that, but it contains proof that the human race is alien, brought here and implanted." Ben, who hadn't gone to church in a while, was raised in a Catholic family. He took what they had just said as an insult to his beliefs.

"How could you possibly know that the artifact revealed that?" Red Feather looked at Ben, and put his hand on his knee, "Have faith my son, and you too shall see the light." Brian, who had been listening to the conversation, yelled back to the group sitting precariously in the rear of the news van. It was filled with studio equipment and not really designed for passengers. "Hey, the cube also indicated that our religions are based loosely on our alien past." Lily looked up at Brian and could see the sincerity in his eyes. She then swung around and asked the old man, "You mentioned a prophecy, what is it?"

"We have a great deal that you will need to know, but now is not the time. Given we are in possession of an artifact that my ancestors most likely based the prophecy upon, I feel it would be better for you to hear it from the source as opposed to playing a ten thousand year old telephone game."

Chapter Ninety-Two

The vote was close, but Dani was sure that Tobiah had pulled it off. Somehow, in a room filled with the most powerful men in the world, he did it, he was able to build enough doubt and hope that he could actually win this small battle. She stood there staring at him with unabashed admiration. He continued to work the room. Even though most of the voters had made up their minds, he was working the individuals whom he thought may lean his way in the end. He walked over to Dani and she began to question him, "How do you know who may go your way?"

The President smiled and winked, "Have you ever heard of John Locke?" She shrugged her shoulders, "It sounds familiar, but I can't place it." He had an extreme depth of knowledge from which he could draw, and he tried to explain, "Some of these folks are followers of Locke and Jefferson. We may be able to use that to our advantage." Dani continued to listen, but didn't really understand what he was talking about. "You see Dani, Locke believed that our ability to reason was more important than anything. This court is attempting to preemptively stop us from making a choice that they see as destructive. That goes against everything they believe in. So if we use it to our advantage, we could get them on our side."

Dani kind of understood, but something struck her as odd. What about the Democrats? She saw him talking to mostly Republicans, and not Democrats, so she asked, "This may be a dumb question, but all the people you talked to seem to be Republicans, why didn't you talk to the Democratic leaders that are here?"

"Dani, the parties as you know them don't really exist. Most of the issues are manufactured to control the masses. They are used as the carrots that get dangled in front of you to induce a desired result. However, there are some divisions that are real. Traditional Democrats believe in Hobbes, as opposed to Locke. You see, Hobbes believed that a human being is a selfish being, hell bent on self destruction. Then, there are the radical Republicans, who are ruled by their moral values and steeped in their skewed view of reality. They work together to keep the masses ignorant and themselves in power." Dani stopped smiling, "Are you saying that Americans are stupid?"

"No Dani. Americans are not stupid. They have been misled, and they allow themselves to languish in ignorance. Anytime there is a threat of credible evidence coming forward that could shed light on what's really going on, it is taken care of. Many times, ruining the sources life and sometimes even ending in death."

Chapter Ninety-Three

Brian, sitting in the news van's front passenger seat, was having a hard time relaxing. The anxiety hadn't been an issue for him before now, because Tiffany had a quality that bestowed trust and calm. Now that there were more people taking her attention, he was left with his downward spiraling thoughts. Lost in a mental prison, analyzing every possible scenario, suddenly he felt a warm hand on his shoulder. He opened his eyes and Tiffany was kneeling down next to him with her hand touching him, "Hey, you OK?" He looked into her deep, chestnut brown eyes and smiled, "I am now." She leaned in and kissed him gently on his forehead, "Everyone is trying to get some rest. I was gonna sit here and lay my head on your leg if that's OK." He smiled coyly and his anxiety lifted away as they both closed their eyes.

Chapter Ninety-Four

Dani and the President made their way towards their respective seats. A five minute warning call had been made. Tobiah, had just finished explaining to Dani, that they would get at least two more chances tomorrow, when they would be able to stall. She couldn't fathom how she had gotten herself involved with such a high level organization. The President didn't make things any easier with his constant references to martyrdom. She had no desire to be a martyr. At thirty-three, she was young, single and not ready to die.

Her worrying was rudely interrupted by Mr. Cash, who sat down next to her. He nudged her with his elbow, "We're both dead. We won't even make it through the night." Dani's heart began to pound. Maybe this was her fate, but she didn't want Mr. Cash to see her so vulnerable, he didn't deserve that. Instead, she looked at him and spoke with contempt, "With all due respect Sir, I would rather die then sell my soul to the devil." She snapped her head back towards Tobiah. This didn't get past the two guards that the President had assigned to her. One of them took out his shortwave communicator. He typed in a message and pressed send. On the other side of the room, the President took a device out of his pocket and read the screen, *"Life just threatened."* He looked back at Dani, who appeared alright. Then, he typed in, *"Take her into office after vote. I'll be there shortly."* The guard knew that there was very little time left, that it could happen at any time. He needed to keep on his toes.

Chapter Ninety-Five

The 9 News van pulled up to a gate that was closed. It indicated that the Window Rock Tribal Park & Veteran's Memorial was closed after 6:00 P.M. Window Rock's ceremonial name means Earth's Center, and it resided at the heart of the Navajo nation. Gavin was the only one awake, so he pulled off the road, turned out the lights and reached back to wake up Lily. In doing so, his shirt brushed up against Tiffany, who was sitting on the ground in between the two front seats, it awakened her. Lily quietly said, "We're here." Lily smiled and Tiffany took control, yelling, "Alright y'all we're here!" Lily reached back and grabbed a box full of battery powered camera lights. "These are really bright and get hot, so be careful." She handed them out to everyone in the van.

"OK, let's go." She flung open the door and jumped out. The whole crew walked around the gate and up the road towards Window Rock. They hadn't turned on any of their lights and the moon was at full mast. This gave the appearance that the desert was glowing in black and white. No one said a word as they walked up towards monument. Red Feather began to hum a chant that intoxicated the scene and brought the huge monolithic structure into focus. The enormous sandstone rock had a massive opening through the center, like a giant window through the mountain. Wes broke the silence with his normal charm, "So, what the hell are we looking for?" Brian answered Wes, "We're not really sure, but we'll know when we see it." Wes then pointed over at a grouping of stucco structures with tile roofs. "What about those buildings?" The old man replied, "That is the Navajo Veterans Memorial and Tribal Park."

"Veterans Memorial?"

"The code talkers that helped the US win the Second World War were Navajo."

"I seem to remember learning that in history class." Tiffany cut in, "I'm surprised that a man like you learned anything." The old man just ignored Tiffany and continued, "If the gate is closed, that means that the last of them has gone home." Brian and Tiffany had already begun to climb the huge structure, moving towards the hole in the center of the rock, for which it was named. They thought this was clearly the only option. Lily, not dressed for mountain climbing, was kicking herself for not bringing a change of clothing and shoes. However, the story required it, so she slid off her six hundred dollar, Jimmy Choo stilettos and followed them up the rock in her bare feet.

Ben sat down and took a deep sigh, the old man sat down beside him. "You OK?" Ben answered while shaking his head from side to side indicating no, "Yes. Just wish my arm was strong enough to let me climb that." Red Feather took out his wooden pipe. It was covered in tribal carvings and wrapped in several places with lengths of leather that had small beads and feathers hanging from them. He packed it and took a few puffs. He held the pipe out to Officer Lovato. As he exhaled, he said, "Ben, the wise man accepts his fate and worries of nothing." Ben looked at the pipe and stuttered, "I, I, I,..." The old man chuckled, "You are a prisoner of your thoughts. You can't possibly see value in the smoke of a plant."

"No, it's just I'm a..." Red Feather took another puff and spoke as he cut Ben off, "...prisoner." Gavin, was standing there without a camera, he wasn't sure what to do. So, he sat down next to the other two and watched, as Wes followed Lily, Brian and Tiffany scaling up the side of the mountain. The old man offered him the pipe and Gavin graciously accepted the gesture.

Chapter Ninety-Six

After another brief but mysterious ceremony, the altar behind the red velvet drapes was revealed, and the voting was called to commence. The altar was an enormous slab of pure white marble. It sat upon a black pyramid with a flattened top, also fashioned of marble. The surface of the snow white slab was covered in blood red candle wax that had been poured over it during the ceremony. A line had been drawn down the center using an embellished dagger that the Emperor carried.

Everyone in the room lined up to cast their votes. There were two lines. The first was a short row of all males. They cast their votes with a ring that they each wore. The longer line had to cast their votes by choosing either a black or white wax seal, and placing it on a piece of scarlet red parchment paper. Dani was blown away to see that the President was in her line. Meaning he didn't have a ring, he was not part of the upper elite. This also meant, that his vote only counted as one, while the "Ring Bearers", as they referred to themselves, counted as two. Each Ring Bearer wore a gold signet ring. They all appeared to be similar in shape, size and color. However, they each bore a symbol unique to the bearer. They placed their votes by leaving the impression of their ring upon the side of the altar with which they chose to align themselves. The only thing Tobiah had going in his favor, was the fact that there were at least four times more non-ring bearers than there were Ring Bearers.

A waiter walked up to Dani with a silver tray full of water bottles. He took one and handed it to each person as he went down the line. After handing one to Dani, she realized how hungry and thirsty she really was and her mouth began to water. Before she could get the bottle to her lips, the body guard confiscated it and replaced it with one of his own. He was not going to let his boss down. Not today, not on the day the President's family was already in danger. Dani said, "Thank you." then, asked, "Can we eat sometime?" The guard whispered in her ear, "As soon as you cast your vote, you will go back to the office and we'll get some food." Dani smiled and rubbed her stomach, "OK." The process went rather quickly. Dani placed her vote, choosing a pure white wax seal. The guard wouldn't allow her to eat the sacrament or drink the wine and escorted her out of the room.

Chapter Ninety-Seven

Once inside the opening of Window Rock, the foursome searched aimlessly for a sign, but nothing could be found. The lights scanned every inch of the rock, but there was no sign from Tiffany's Father. It was evident that Lily was distracted, and not really helping the search. Tiffany questioned her, "Hey, Ms. Levine, are you really looking or are you too preoccupied with looking good?" Lily had been thinking about the story and working on possible ways to introduce the piece. She looked at Tiffany and apologized, "I'm sorry. I realize that this is important." Tiffany was taken aback by the apology and pleasantly surprised with Lily's attitude. She had heard really bad things about Lily, but she had just made a positive impression.

Brian walked back over to the edge and yelled down at the old man, "Red Feather, you know any significance to this place?" Brian shined his light down at the Túhikya, Gavin and Ben. The old man yelled back up, "The spring is the giver of life." Brian thought to himself. *Why does he have to speak in prose?* However, he had noticed a water puddle near the backside of the rock's opening. He hurried over towards the spot. Lily, Tiffany and Wes all joined him around the water hole. It looked like a puddle, but when they shined their bright lights down at the sparkling water, they gasped at what they saw. There in the water, was a glowing key, encircled by rocks precisely laid out to spell, *"QÖMVI"*, along with a new set of clues like the ones Brian and Tiffany had found at Mesa Verde;

Clue #6
EC 1/9x – 39.5 (35, -36)

Tiffany knelt down and reached her hand out to grab the key. She nearly fell in, so Brian held her other hand as she slowly submerged her fingers into the water and clasped the diamond shaped key. As she took it out of the water, Wes asked, "Is that stuff safe to touch? I mean, the old man and the cube both alluded to the idea that it was a power source. If its uranium or plutonium, we could all get sick or even die." Brian looked up at Wes as he pulled Tiffany up to her feet. "From the work we were doing in Professor Gerardo's lab, I believe that this source does not contain radioactive isotopes." Tiffany scowled at Wes, "That means that no, you won't get sick."

Lily pulled out her phone and took a photo of the rocks lit up under the water's surface. She asked, "What about the words and numbers, do they have any significance?" Brian answered her, as Tiffany walked towards the edge of the cliff to climb down, "Those, my dear, are our next clues."

"Don't we need to write them down? "

"Tiffany has a photographic memory, but I'm sure your photo will help." They all reached the edge and looked out over the desert horizon. The moon was shining, and all the lights were off. They could see for miles and the night sky was filled with millions of twinkling stars. Tiffany was inspired and invigorated by the view, "One step closer." Suddenly, her foot gave way and she slid over the edge.

Chapter Ninety-Eight

It seemed to Dani that she had been sitting in the President's dark, dirty office for more than an hour. Mr. Tobiah finally entered the room and Dani sprang from her chair, a customary show of respect for anyone of his stature. The President spoke to her, "Dani, you don't need to stand for me. You have proven today, that even a secretary can bring the elite to their knees." Dani sat back down and thought about what he had just said. The sense of pride made her smile and sit up straight, "So now what?" The President explained how there was a recess that would last until 6:00 A.M. That would give them about six hours to get some rest. He pointed at a couple of military cots with olive drab blankets on them. Dani took a deep breath, but knew that this was the safest place for the night.

She really wanted to know more details about the President's plan. "I realize that we have time to rest, but what is the plan?" He looked at Dani and knew she deserved to know, being that it directly affected her. Right now the most powerful man in the world really needed this little secretary, so he explained to her, "The reason they don't mind calling a recess, is because there are assassins on the trail, and by six o'clock in the morning, the couple will likely be dead and everything will go back to status quo. However, I think that there is hope. See, I may not really be the head of this country, however very few people really know that. So, when the entire plan went into action I was asked to give out the orders. I made sure that one of the three assassins was a true, blue American. One that has a record of doing what is right, even if it's against orders. His name is Wesley Grove, and he may be able to help us."

"How are the assassins going to find them in the middle of the desert?"

"There are actually four similar devices that have been found throughout history. On the top of all four, there is a special compass, one that only points to the location of the other artifacts when they are activated." Dani had seen a compass before, but never one that could find an object. "How is that possible?"

"That answer has escaped our scientists, who have failed to recreate the intricate device, even after x-raying it and reverse engineering it several times. After testing one of the compass needles, they realized that the metal used was not of this world."

"So it's true, we're not alone in the universe?"

"No, and the material that the cube is made of is most definitely extraterrestrial. They have found that one gram of the metal the keys are made of could power the United States for decades. The problem is we don't have the technology to do it. But we did figure out, that the compass only works when the device is activated. In the year 1962, one of the devices was activated in Cuba. This set off a chain of events that eventually led to the Cuban Missile Crisis. The compass on our artifact, that had been part of our country's secret from the very beginning, suddenly sprang to life. The CIA was convinced that communism was an alien take over.   JFK, made the decision to allow the Soviet Union to procure their own cube. That decision alone sealed his fate, and put in motion a true coup d'état after his assassination. The president became more of a figure head, but I digress. My plan is to call Wesley and ask him to help me. As long as he's in, I'm sure they can make it through the night."

"What are you waiting for?"

"You're right." He picked up a small cell phone and dialed. The phone on the other end rang.

Chapter Ninety-Nine

As the rock gave way, Tiffany slid off the side of the mountain and the key flew up into the air. Wes nimbly sprang into action and dove, catching Tiffany's wrist as she dangled off the side of the forty foot cliff. Brian also dove at the same time, catching the key. The moment was interrupted by the ringing of a phone. Wes pulled Tiffany up quickly and grabbed his cell phone from his pocket, "Hello." On the other side of the line was the President of the United States. He quickly stood up straight and answered like he was standing at attention, "Yes, Sir, I understand Sir, no problem Sir. Yes, they're here. I will Sir. Thank you Sir." Wes's eyes lit up as he closed his phone. Tiffany and Brian were still brushing off their clothes, when Lily asked, "Who was that?"

"That was the President of the United States, and he has asked that I..." Tiffany, assuming she knew what he was going to say interrupted, "You get rid of us." Wes gave a harsh look at Tiffany and continued, "No. That I do everything in my power to ensure your safety, and wished us all good luck." Taken aback, Lily asked, "So, the President is on our side? Is he going to send reinforcements?" Wes shook his head sadly, "He said we were on our own, and that there are only five compasses out there. I'm now in possession of three out of the five, and I believe that one of the five is on the artifact itself." Brian questioned, "So there's only one compass out there that can still track us?"

"That and the sleeper." Tiffany, still not a fan of Wes interjected, "So, we know at least two more attackers are coming after us, great."

"I'm the best in the business. I assure you we're going to make it." With that, he was done talking and they started to descend back down the mountain. Brian and Lily looked at Tiffany. Brian spoke, "Red Feather said we needed him, maybe this is why." She grimaced, "OK, but that pit bull needs a short leash." They all chuckled as they descended down the dark face, trying not to miss step. After a couple of minutes they all reached the bottom together. Lily was surprised to find Ben and Gavin were involved in a pipe ceremony around a small campfire they had made. The old man looked at all four and asked them to sit. They sat and joined in the ceremony.

Lily had no idea why everyone was doing this, when the pipe got to her she did not accept it. The Túhikya said to her, "You need to purify the mind, or your story will be lost." She was surprised that he knew her desires. But a man of his stature in the Hopi community could read people's expressions. She was a typical American, lost in emotions, a slave to her thoughts and desires. "So how, or what do I do?" she asked. Red Feather explained the ritual again and she followed it exactly. When the pipe reached him he spoke, "Not everyone will make it through this journey, but if we accept what the artifact reveals tonight, we shall all meet again."

Chapter One Hundred

Captain Barba was standing in the middle of the station commanding his troops, when suddenly a paramilitary group came storming in from every entry point. They quickly took over the station without firing a shot. Captain Barba was knocked out with the butt of an AR-15 assault rifle. More than twenty-five of them stormed through the station to make sure there was no one hiding. As Captain Barba came to, he heard one of them speak on the radio, "All secure."

He faded in and out of consciousness, but clearly recognized the federal agents returning through the door. Special Agent Pope reached down and lifted the Captain's head up, "Did you think you could use our satellites without us noticing? You led us right to them and implicated yourselves in the process." He dropped the head. "Everyone in the station will spend the rest of their lives in a cell."

Sandy, who had been brought out of the server room with Nak, was sitting at her desk, with her hands under the table. One of the soldiers took exception and ordered her to put her hands up. She did, and she was holding a cell phone. He grabbed it, looked at the screen and yelled to Special Agent Swanson, "Sir, I think we have a problem." He walked the phone over to the special agent in charge.

He snatched the phone and read the message out loud, *"Destroy all cells. The feds are tracking."* He was obviously not very happy, he and Special Agent Pope walked over into the break room. Sandy could not make out what they were saying, but she knew it wasn't good.

When they came back into the room, Special Agent Pope said, "Bag 'em." A burlap sack was harshly shoved over Sandy's head scratching her cheek and her arms were bound behind her back. She heard screams and scuffles, and although she couldn't see, she knew they were taking everybody. She didn't understand. *How in this great, free society can this be happening?* Before today, she had never questioned her country, but now, everything was different. Now she started to see the illusion of freedom eroding away before her very eyes.

Chapter One Hundred One

Ben had no idea why anyone was calling his phone, or that his phone was now a bulls eye on his back. He turned it off out of respect for the Túhikya. The group was about to insert the key they had just found into the artifact. When Tiffany placed it into the cube, a hologram of an Indian chief popped up and introduced himself to Ben, "Hello." He morphed into an Aztec chief. Just as it had before, every time it spoke to someone new, its appearance changed. "I am Kasicote." He swung to Lily, morphing into a young Hebrew woman, "Pleasure to meet you." Then it swung to Gavin and morphed into a Hawaiian kapuna, "Aloha." Without notice, it changed from a head to a full figure standing above the cube facing Brian and Tiffany, "So many questions. Ask." Tiffany spoke, "You said…" The cube cut her off, "I know what I said. What is the question?" Before Tiffany could get her question out Brian asked, "What about our religions is true?"

The figure sighed, "Now, that's a question. There was indeed one creator or inventor if you will. He invented the cloning technology that led to the human race, and is considered to be your creator. It was intended for all implanted colonies to have a strong moral code, which to us meant treating each other with respect. The ability to reason, we thought would be enough to help fight off the aggressive nature of the primate. The mixture of our DNA and that of the Neanderthal did not have the desired effect. There is an afterlife, but the simplicity escapes all of your religions..." Lily interrupted, "How would you know anything about our religions?" He didn't skip a beat, "This planet is an observatory, and every visiting sightseer is required to leave a digital dump of the information collected. You can think of me as a filing cabinet, or desk top computer for that matter." He swung back to Brian and continued, "The afterlife is simple, but the nature of the primate kept interfering. So, about two thousand years ago, a council was formed. They allowed for some of the genetic markers in select humans to be triggered. This gave them a unique connection with what we call the life force, or the power. You may refer to it as God, Allah or Jehovah, all different names for the same entity. Some of the individuals made inroads for a brief time. However, man always seems to interpret what's been said for his own selfish gains. For example, one of our edicts, given to you from that failed attempt was judge not lest ye be judged. We all know how well you have listened to that. Then, there's the concept of turn the other cheek. Your religions are all based on simple decency, and yet every one of them is far reaching in its attacks and judgments." It turned and looked out across the open desert, "We have incoming."

The hologram disappeared back into the cube and Wes jumped up, "Shit!" He reached into his pocket, grabbed his cell phone and smashed it on the ground. Ben turned on his phone to find a message from Sandy. He promptly smashed it on the ground and looked at Wes, "They're tracking our phones. What are we going to do?"

"Give me your coats." He put the coats around a couple of posts, placing Gavin's hat on top of one of them. "Now everyone, off that way, lie down in the mud and get it all over you. They'll have infrared and the mud will help mask where you're at." Brian asked, "What are you going to do?"

"Not sure. Just get in the mud." They all ran over and started covering themselves with the sticky mud from the spring water runoff that had pooled at the bottom of the rock. Ben and Red Feather stayed with Wes. Wes was not happy about this, but he knew that the old man needed some help. Now, more than ever he also needed some luck.

The faint sounds of a helicopter were approaching quickly, but at this point there was still no visual. Wes climbed back up inside the rock hastily. Neither Ben, nor the old man could make the climb, he yelled back, "You'll have five seconds once we have visual. If you're not in the mud, you probably won't make it." Ben looked at Red Feather and politely asked, "Can you make that run?" The Túhikya continued to sit, never showing any worry or panic. He looked at Ben, "I have no intention of running. My spirit already walks in both worlds." Ben wasn't sure what he was talking about, but out of the corner of his eye he saw the light of an Apache attack helicopter approaching quickly. Ben turned and looked at Red Feather, "Let's go!" The old man winked, "Leave me. This is my destiny."

Ben took off running across the parking lot as fast as he could, as he dove into the mud puddle he could see the explosion starting by the campfire. When he came up for air, bushes were burning and the helicopter was circling above the site, looking for survivors. He looked up at and saw Wes flying through the air. He landed inside of the chopper and within seconds it was careening down towards the ground. Ben, Lily, Tiffany, Brian and Gavin peered out of the mud in astonishment at the wreckage.

Chapter One Hundred Two

The Emperor's elegant quarters were dripping with opulence. There were pieces of art, crystal chandeliers, luxurious fabrics and items gilded with gold everywhere you looked. It was apparent that this was the dwelling of an extremely wealthy person. A minor cheer filled the entertainment room. The top leaders had just received the call they were waiting for, the target had been hit. The Emperor actually jumped up off of the ground and pumped his fists in the air. Everyone in the room felt that they had saved the world. Their exuberance was short lived, as another interruption came onto the huge flat screen, hanging on the wall in front of them. They saw a large, red, blinking "X". The Emperor's son had the remote in his hand and clicked a button, opening a pop up window, with a man in fatigues. "Sir, our conformation on the hit may have been premature." The mood quickly changed and the Emperor erupted, "What are you saying?"

"Just after conformation, the chopper went down. So, we assume that some of them survived." The look on the group of elite's faces was that of sheer horror, and what former President Clint Williams asked froze the room, "So, where's the backup?" They all stared at the television waiting for an answer. The soldier looked uncomfortably off camera, and a second man stepped into view, "Mr.

Firewater here. Sir, I'm sorry to inform you, but we we're not prepared for any domestic events, as this is the first time we have ever been used in that capacity. Most of our resources have been tied up in Iraq and Afghanistan. So, only one Apache was sent in." Hyde Jr., the Emperor's son asked, "Do you have any idea how many survived?"

"No Sir, but we do have a reconnaissance team on the way." The Emperor cut in, "What about the two assassins we sent in?" The man's face turned somber, "We lost contact with them shortly after their initial report. We can only assume that they are dead."

"Make sure to update us when the reconnaissance team confirms the results." He motioned to his son to turn off the video link. He sat down and placed his head in his hands.

Chapter One Hundred Three

Ben and Brian both sprinted towards the wreckage. Tiffany, Lily and Gavin went to see if Red Feather had made it. When Brian got to the downed helicopter, Wes popped out, stretching his neck from left to right. Ben arrived shortly after, "Are you OK?"

"Ship shape Sir." He jumped out of the helicopter. "We gotta go now." He looked around, "Where are the girls?" Brian pointed up at the monument. Wes looked up, to see Lily and Tiffany searching the grounds for remains. Their facial expressions made Wes realize that something was wrong. He sprinted towards them with Brian and Ben in tow, stopping in the middle of the huge blast area. The scorched earth smelled like a campfire and still smoldered from the explosion. The girls looked at the boys and shrugged their shoulders. Tiffany walked up to Brian, "No trace. It completely vaporized him." The tears in her eyes surprised Brian, but he was eager to help. He opened his arms and Tiffany buried her head in Brian's chest, "I just don't understand how our own government can be doing this."

Lily walked over to Gavin and pulled on his sleeve, motioning with her head to go with her. They walked just out of earshot. "The old man is dead right? How much footage were you able to get with the hidden camera?" Gavin smiled, "I think all of it."

Chapter One Hundred Four

Sandy knew that she was in a vehicle, and she knew that she was lying next to at least two of her co-workers, but that was it. Her world had been ripped away from under her feet. She felt an odd sense of calm in the face of such incredible circumstances. She grinned, knowing that no one could possibly see her smile though the bag that was over her head. She thought about it, and came to the realization that there wasn't an out for this one. There was no Habeas Corpus, no innocent until proven guilty. For the first time in her life, she felt the shadow of death creep over her. She thought about all the things she would miss, all the things she wanted to tell Ben. She couldn't believe that she had never really told him how she felt, how she longed to be his wife, and mother of his children. "Not now, not ever." She repeated the phrase over and over again as she sobbed into her burlap mask, until she was startled by the voice of Captain Barba, "Hold it together. We'll pull through."

A loud thud came as the butt of a rifle hit the Captain's head, knocking him out. Another voice madly scolded the Captain, "You ain't pulling through shit. You're all enemy combatants, and will be dealt with as such." Sandy had a renewed sense of confidence. She was angered by the man's assertion. She made up her mind right there, that she would see Ben again.

Chapter One Hundred Five

Wes was the last person to get in the news van. When he sat down, their mood was somber, so the marine in him came out. "OK troops. Just because we've been hit doesn't mean were down. Buck up, and get your heads in the game. If we work together, all of us will survive, and God willing, the President will save this country." Ben reached out to Wes, and the two shook hands. They didn't have to say a word. The handshake alone was a show of respect, one that expressed how much they needed each other, without having to say it.

Brian looked at Tiffany and leaned in, "He's right. Red Feather even said it." Tiffany looked at Ben and Wes, then up to the front where Lily and Gavin were sitting, staring back at her. Somehow, all of them were looking to Tiffany to be their glue. Three days ago, she was an unknown archaeologist. Today, she was the glue that could save the world. She smiled at Brian, leaned forward and kissed him softly on the forehead, "They'll have to rewrite the history books when we're done tomorrow." Gavin turned around, and asked, "Where to?" Brian looked at Tiffany. She looked at the map and graph that he had in his hands. He pointed at the name Chaco Canyon and turned the map around so it faced her. She examined the map then yelled up to Gavin, "West on 256." The van sped off into the darkness.

Chapter One Hundred Six

The little wind up alarm clock was sitting on an old, metal desk that weighed as much as a compact car, it began to ring loudly. The blaring sound pierced Dani's dream, waking her back into reality, a reality that didn't seem possible forty-eight hours ago. She was quite certain, that if today's events were to become public, no one would believe it. She rolled over on her uncomfortable cot and came face to face with the President whose own cot was barely a foot away. He leaned over and pressed the off button. He flashed one of his famous toothy grins as he sat up. "Well, its 5:00 A.M., we have an hour to have breakfast and get ready for the morning. You…" He stood up and walked over to the door as he continued to talk, "…may need to be very careful today. The powers that be won't stop at one attempt."

Dani smiled and sat up, swinging her legs over the side of the cot. The President opened the door and leaned out. She could hear him asking one of his guards to get them breakfast. She slipped on her Payless shoes, reminding her again of how ironic it was that she was here. She got up, and did her best to straighten out her wrinkled suit skirt and shirt. *It would really be nice if I had my bag right now. Too bad Mr. Cash is such a jerk.* When the President came back into the room she asked, "What do you think is going to happen?" The distress in her voice was fully noted by the President, who quickly confronted her with some good old positive thinking. "I believe that today could be the day that we take our country back, no longer beholden to the corruption and coercion of the wealthy. After today, Dani, your name will be echoed throughout history classes across our great nation, and once again, we will be a true beacon of hope." Dani smiled wholeheartedly and a warming sensation began to grow inside of her.

Chapter One Hundred Seven

No one in the van could sleep even though it was almost 5:00 A.M., and they hadn't been to bed all night. At this point, their bodies were running on pure adrenaline. Ben asked Tiffany, "Can we turn the cube on?"

"Why?" she asked. He looked quizzically at Brian, "You guys aren't curious? My mind hasn't stopped thinking about what that thing said." Tiffany reached down between Brian's legs and grabbed the green backpack. She carefully unzipped it and took out the artifact, then gently placed it on the floorboard between them. As soon as she put both keys they had found back onto it, it sprang to life, "New question please." This time, it appeared as a Buddhist monk, sitting cross legged. Tiffany asked, "What am I the key to?" The cube fired back, "Don't ask questions you know the answer to, next question." Ben spoke up, "How do we know, that you are what you say you are?"

The Buddhist monk quickly flew across the van and stood next to Ben. The hologram looked real, but was able to easily change its size. He held up his hand, "Please remove your jacket." Ben took off his jacket gingerly, revealing a bloody stain on his left shoulder. "Now your shirt." the cube prompted. He pulled off his shirt and his bandages, exposing the stitches that had just been placed there twenty-four hours earlier. The monk raised his hand and set it on Ben's shoulder. Ben felt as if a real hand had just been placed upon him. The monk directed Ben, "Focus on something you love." Five seconds went by. The monk removed his hand from the wound. The van swerved, Wes, Tiffany and Lily all let out audible gasps and Brian exclaimed, "Holy shit!" Ben looked down, and the entire wound was healed, it was completely gone. He looked at the hologram and was totally speechless.

The monk retracted back to his sitting position, floating above the cube, "Any other questions?" Gavin yelled back, "Bruddah man, how the hell'd you do that?" He rotated around then answered, "The energy in the magnetic fields of a galactic object, like a planet let's say, can be used for many purposes. One is the art of healing. Ironically, this was one of the few things we tried to pass on, but somehow this time around you've gone backwards. You're living well under one hundred years of age. It's sad really, that your ancestor's knowledge has been lost. Time's up." The hologram disappeared.

Chapter One Hundred Eight

The ancient ceremonies and rituals, reminded Dani of a mixture of suspense film and the few experiences she'd had as a child, at her family's Catholic Church. She made her way to the new seat that Tobiah had arranged. He told her, that her old boss and the head honchos would stop at nothing until she was dead. His words echoed through her mind, drowning out all of the gibberish and commotion she was surrounded by. She visualized the President saying over and over again, "We are our country's only hope."

The loud, cracking knock of the gavel snapped her mind back into focus. The Emperor entered the room. His demeanor spoke volumes as to the result of the vote. He was confident, and his head was held high, he didn't waste time as he stepped up to the podium and began to speak, "The vote is in, and it is clear that our errand boy was misguided and distracting... The measure has failed. Now, back to the question on the floor, do we kill them with our assassins, or do we use the sleeper's suitcase bomb?"

A short break in speech, gave the Emperor's son the chance to ask to be heard. This former president may have been the worst president of all time. Yet, here, he was a hero, the final piece in a fifty year long plan. He stood up, "I respectfully request an opportunity, to fill in the room on the latest intelligence. I feel that one of our options is off the table." A quick second came from the former Vice President, whose radical use of fear to procure popular opinion was something of legend.

Hyde Jr. rose and offered the aforementioned information, "People of the court, you should know that the assassins have either been killed, or decided to switch sides. We found out at 3:00 A.M., and were able to get a fix on them. We quickly attempted to neutralize the problem, but they survived. To make matters even worse, they have been joined by others, including a police officer and a local Denver reporter named Lily Levine, and right now we have no idea where they're at." He sat down and the Emperor spoke, "In light of this, I'm calling for an immediate vote on the use of the sleeper cell. Before they're able to activate the device and expose the truth, causing fatal cracks in the foundation that our society is built on."

Dani was terrified, after the vote failed, she suddenly felt very cold and nauseas. The hope she had for humanity was crushed by a room full of fat cats who feasted on the pain and misfortune of others. Each word that was said felt like a deadly blow to her inflated perception of human decency.

Chapter One Hundred Nine

The news van pulled into the dirt parking lot at Chaco Culture National Historic Park in New Mexico. The sun was just cresting the horizon, casting a coral red hue which engulfed the landscape. Tiffany stepped out of the van and looked up, the view made her forget how tired she was. The crisp morning air rejuvenated her entire crew. As Ben stepped out of the van, he asked Tiffany, "Why did the clues point here or more aptly how?" Tiffany looked at Brian, "You want to explain?" Brian started to talk, while all five listened and began walking towards the entrance.

"Once we figured out that he used the basic algebraic equation for slope-intercept to encode where each key was, it was pretty simple. Then, all we had to do was determine that the Four Corners monument was the Point of Origin for our graph. At that point, we laid the coordinate graph over the map of the area and voila. The last clue had an equation and a set of coordinates. When graphed, they create a line with an end point that lands us here." Lily interrupted, "What about the word Qömvi? It was there too. Do you know what it meant?" Tiffany looked at her with the disgust that Lily was used to, but had to look back quickly and nearly fell. She answered with disdain in her voice. "No. We don't, and there has been a word at all four mapped locations that didn't fit. I have a hunch, that the fifth word will show us."

Chaco Canyon, much like Mesa Verde, covers a very large geographic area. However, the large, curving Pueblo Bonito, which was fashioned in the shape of a hunter's bow, was by far the most famous structure in the park. It was also built by the same clan that had built the Sun Temple. So, Tiffany decided it was as good place to start. No one said another word as they approached the pueblo, until Wes asked, "So, why these places? Why did your Dad pick these places?" Brian interceded, "Well, we think that he picked places that all have ancient connections to the Puebloans and their depictions of Star People." Wes had a confused look on his face, "Star People?"

"I know. Most modern scientists have the same reaction, but after getting this artifact and connecting the dots, it's the only possible scenario. Our people were planted here by Star People." Tiffany interrupted Brian, "It's even possible that the legend of the Ant People may be true." Brian continued, "It may be related. I find it hard to believe, that it can't be considering..." Wes looked at Ben and asked, "I'm lost, Ant People?" Brian kept going, "In 1909, an explorer named G.E. Kincaid stumbled upon ruins in the Grand Canyon, that he claimed prove the existence of an alien race. He believed the ruins predated the Egyptian civilization or even Babylon. Kincaid described in detail the various chambers throughout the complex, which he claimed contained several hundred rooms. *The Phoenix Gazette* even ran a story on it in April of that year, but most scientists and historians discredited it, however the story has prevailed as the legend of the Ant People.

Tiffany cut in, "But, this may not be related to that at all. Although, I will admit there are some striking similarities. The key is, we just don't know and even with this artifact, it still needs to be tested and verified."

Lily asked her questioningly, "Didn't you just see it heal Officer Lovato? If that's not verified, I don't know what is!" Brian again buffered, "As scientists and archaeologists, until the carbon dating is done, we have become very weary of forgeries and fakes. But, this is something that I've never heard of, so the likely hood is pretty small that it's fake." Wes added, "If it wasn't real, none of us would still be here."

They walked up to a towering adobe wall, the plaque on the adjacent trail explained the various pictographs painted everywhere, but Tiffany and Brian weren't interested in history lessons. They walked up to the paintings and started scanning the area for anything unusual. Nothing looked out of place, no extra graphite, they were stumped. Then, Lily pointed to the plaque, "Hey. Didn't you guys say basic algebra?" Ben and Wes stared down at the plaque. Wes spoke first, "What do you know." Tiffany and Brian ran over to find another clue;

Clue #7
QÖÖTSA

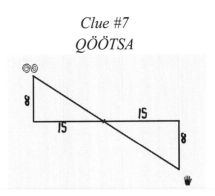

The group all looked up at the adobe wall and back down at the plaque. Sure enough, there wasn't a clue on the wall it was on the plaque. "What's it mean?" Ben asked. Brian answered, "Looks like a map." Lily interjected, "Using the Pythagorean Theorem." Surprised, everyone looked at her. "I had a really good eighth grade math teacher." They all chuckled as Brian did the math on a piece of paper;

$$A^2 + B^2 = C^2$$
$$8^2 + 15^2 = C^2$$
$$64 + 225 = C^2$$
$$\sqrt{289} = C$$
$$C = 17$$

He plugged 17 into the two missing values in the diagram, after adding them together, he got 34.

"OK. Thirty-four steps from the wall." Tiffany ran over and stood at the wall facing them, "Which way should I go?" Brian looked down at the diagram, put his finger on the corner and whispered to himself, "Ninety degrees, so half of that is forty-five degrees to your, left." He knew he was right, and this time said it out loudly, "Forty-five degrees on your left side." She started to walk, counting each step as she got closer and closer to another wall. On her thirty-fourth step, she came face to face with another one of the adobe walls that created the pueblo. Right at eye level, it looked as if one of the exposed stones had been cut out and replaced like a piece of a puzzle. She worked her fingers into the cracks around the stone and started to wiggle it free. Everyone was right behind her as she removed the stone. Wes asked, "Are you going to reach in?" She looked around, took a deep breath and stuck her hand into the hole.

Chapter One Hundred Ten

Dani had not heard a word for more than twenty minutes. The mouths moved, their faces showed emotion and passion, but for Dani, the world had already stopped. *These people cannot be real. How can they smile and laugh? How dare they?* In her mind, the room was like a fish bowl, and she was watching as the sharks surrounded her. Her heart began to beat at a faster pace, the tightness in her chest started to scare her. This only exasperated the situation, heightening her anxiety. Without even noticing, everyone around Dani got up. She just sat there, sulking, wandering aimlessly through the nightmare playing in her head. It wasn't until the President pinched her, that she sprang back to reality.

"Ouch." She grimaced. The President apologized, "I know it seems like all is lost, but you need to be strong. I have forces working on the outside too." He got down close and looked straight into her eyes, "Dani, your country needs you. I need you. Given enough time and real exposure, I still think we can fix this." Dani's face changed, as though something had clicked, "Can you get a message to a pager?" The President laughed, "Are you feeling OK?"

"Well, my friend is the one they said was with the couple. I know she always carries a pager."

"What do you mean your friend?"

"Didn't they say, that they think they're with a reporter named Lily Levine?" He nodded his head, acknowledging that she was right. "Well, my college roommate was Lily Levine, and she has a pager that is registered to MSNBC. She works as an on call journalist for anything major in her area."

"I thought she was a reporter for a local Denver station?"

"She's third on the rotation at her station, behind two younger girls that came in and bumped her out. As you can imagine it was..." He stopped her, "OK. So what's the number and what should we say?"

"Broadcast now and save yourself, President Tobiah and Dani Long Legs." He pulled out a notepad and pen and wrote down the information. Then, he called over one of his bodyguards and gave him the folded up piece of paper. After explaining the instructions, the man turned and walked briskly towards the exit. The President knelt back down, "OK. It's done. Now let's pray she gets it."

Chapter One Hundred Eleven

Tiffany screamed a blood curdling scream that had very little emotion, and even less believability. She looked back and grinned. Apparently, she was the only one who found this funny. So, she decided to change the subject. She pulled out the next key. No one said a word. They all came together and sat down in a circle. Brian placed the cube in between them. Ben, pulled the peace pipe out of his jacket, it had been in the hip sack he was holding, when he dove away from the bombs that had killed Red Feather. He reached in and grabbed a pinch of tobacco, placed it in the pipe and quickly sparked the ceremony. Each of them briefly asked for forgiveness and partook of the pipe. When it reached Tiffany, she knew what she had to do. She placed the newest key into the cube just as she exhaled. The cube sprang to life.

This time it was different. There was no head, just diagrams and pictures, hundreds of them, a virtual filing cabinet. Tiffany and Brian instantly knew what they were looking at. "Oh my…" Tiffany finished his sentence, "…God. Do you guys know what we're looking at?" Wes quickly answered, "No." Ben, Gavin and Lily shook their heads to acknowledge the same. Tiffany explained, "These are all either famous archaeological sites, or representations of different petroglyphs, pictographs and other ancient markings from all over the world. But that's not what makes this special. If you look at it from this angle, the same basic shape or markings from various sites throughout the world are all layered one behind another hundreds of times, and every time the image is identical. It's almost like an entire stack of transparency sheets all aligning with the same image in the same spot, but naturally. Meaning, the answers, they've always been here. We just never connected the dots. Here, look at this one. In Giza, this underground labyrinth looks remarkably like the Hopi Spider Woman, who you see behind it here. And this one," she walked right through the Great Pyramid and Hopi Spider Woman, to point at Stone Henge, "You see, Stone Henge is the same as the file behind it, the Mayan Calendar." She whirled around and pointed up to a row cascading down towards them from the sky, "Look, up there, every location we've been to, has a pictograph of Star People that match up, and they line up with pictographs from all over the globe. There must be a thousand, from every civilization that has ever existed." Brian was feeding off of her excitement, "This is the story of man, by man, with no revisions or moral over tones, the true history. Look, look at the chronology, the precision, there are no missing gaps." Tiffany interrupted, "If the cube was right, then this is only one of four cubes, meaning that it's only one quarter of the true history of man."

Gavin, lost in thought, was thinking that this would be his best chance to win a cinematography award. He couldn't believe he was getting all of this on his hard drive. Wes interrupted Tiffany, "Didn't the cube say something about other planets, each having nine worlds?"

"You're right, but from what I understand, and Brian correct me if I'm wrong, our species is unique to this planet. We were hybrid, or crossed between the Neanderthal and the alien. So, our history is really only relevant in the first three worlds before this one."

Suddenly, the filing system shrank into a much smaller area. It moved to Tiffany's right side and another three systems appeared. To her left, in front of her was world number three. She quickly ran her fingers through the digital information as if there were true folders in a filing cabinet hanging in front of her. The files reacted in a life like manner. Tiffany went to the very back and grabbed the last file. She pulled it up in front of her face. She moved through the hundreds of pictures and pictographs before she came to a very familiar sight. She repeated this process three times, once in each of the file systems and each time she discovered that the world ended in destruction. She was so visibly upset, that Brian stepped in to take over, "Look at this Ben. Have you ever heard of Atlantis?" Wes smirked and added, "Everyone's heard of Atlantis."

"The third world here, look at what they called their planet." Lily almost peed herself, "Did we just find Atlantis?" Brian looked at Tiffany, who was trying to hold back the emotion. "Yeah, I think we might have. What do you think Tiffany? Do think we just found Atlantis?" She reined in her emotions and gathered her thoughts. No one rushed her. They all seemed to understand how hard the last couple of days had been on her. "Well, yes. I do think that we may have indeed found Atlantis. But I'm also afraid to tell you, that none of the worlds lasted longer than

253

the year 2038 as we know it." Lily asked, "Like a dooms day prediction, 2012 and all that?"

Her question prompted a file in each of the four world's databases to jump out and line up in front of Lily. She opened one to find a planetary map of constellations, the same one for all four worlds. "What does this mean?" Brian got up, walked over and offered, "Maybe I can help." He reached down, grabbed the virtual file from world number three, he pulled out the three dimensional map of the stars, for the date December 21, 2012. "Yes. This is the phenomenon, where the world, the sun and the center of the universe will all align. It's happened in all of the first three worlds." Wes asked, "Did it destroy them?"

"No. But each time, it started or sparked an age of great destruction." No one said a word. Brian walked back and sat down. Tiffany sat down as well, while above them was hovering, an infinite amount of information. It could literally take a lifetime to go through these files, and yet they were quickly able to deduce that life here is far different than any of them had ever been able to imagine.

Suddenly, a beep went off, breaking the silence, and the virtual library vanished. Wes asked, "What was that?" Again a beep sounded, three times, Lily knew what it was, "Oh, no." She reached into her jacket and pulled out a pager. Wes was angry, "I thought we destroyed all of our phones?" Lily turned bright red and her cheeks got warm, "Honestly, I forgot I had this."

"Give it here. I'll take care of it." She looked at the screen, "Hold on. It's from the President. Look." She handed it to Gavin and he couldn't believe it. It read, *"Broadcast now and save yourself, President Tobiah and*

Dani Long Legs." Wes needed answers, "How can we expose it?" Lily and Gavin both said in unison, "TV."

One Hundred Twelve

Sandy's head hit the ground hard as she was drug rapidly across an open grass area. *Where?* That was the question in her mind. Where were they and how could she escape? She was swung around on to her stomach, the handcuffs dug into her wrists causing sharp pain. A voice yelled, "Get up on your knees and hold your hands up. Those that sit back down or drop their hands die. Everyone here understand?" A voice she couldn't place asked, "Don't we get a phone call?" A gun shot rang out and a thud shortly followed. The voice called out, "Any questions?" It was dead silent, and that's when she heard it, the rail road. *Now, where are we?*

Chapter One Hundred Thirteen

The six of them finally made it to the top of the pueblo, at the apex of the 'D' shaped crescent. They needed to be at the highest point they could in order to use the uplink that Lily and Gavin had. Like the cube had suggested, they linked their video equipment directly into the artifact. This would allow them to stream to every electrical device in the world which produced sound. When they got everything set up, it was nearly 10:00 A.M., and the sun was beating down upon them. Tiffany took out the cube, and inserted the three keys they had found into place.

The head sprang to life and quickly pointed out, "Until you complete the keys and trigger the storage device, I can only reveal so much." Lily winked at Gavin and answered, "Sir, if you can do what you say you can, then Gavin and I will take care of the rest. The only thing that I ask is that you don't make me look like Geraldo Rivera, with that whole Al Capone thing."

"Geraldo Rivera, Al Capone?"

"Never mind, just hope this works. Quiet on the set, in five, four, three,... Hello, I'm Lily Levine, live from Chaco Canyon...." all over the world, every electronic device that could was either showing or echoing what was being said, "...in New Mexico. I am here with renowned archaeologist, Dr. Tiffany Gerardo, and her crew." The camera panned to show Tiffany, Brian, Ben and Wes. "Today, this group discovered, what in Dr. Gerardo's words, will change the history books." She looked at Tiffany, and the camera zoomed in on a statuesque woman. The world was captivated, and thanks to the cube every broadcast was individualized, speaking in the language of the viewers.

"Tell me, Dr. Gerardo, what have you found?" She took a deep breath and hoped what they agreed she would say was going to work, "Well, we believe we have found proof of a creator."

"Are you saying that you may have proof of God?"

"Yes, in a manner of speaking, we may have indeed found proof of God."

"Well folks, you heard it here first. For the next five hours, we will be presenting you with prerecorded evidence, and you will follow us as we solve the final piece of the puzzle. That's right folks, stay tuned live as we show you proof of our creator."

Gavin pushed play, and the hard drive that he had been recording with began to play. The device was new, and he was so glad that he had gone ahead and purchased it. It was similar to an IPod phone, but it's was an IEditor, giving the user the power to take video, edit and publish professional, DVD quality movies. It was the latest in technology for techies and news photographers. Lily was also glad he had it, so they could use it to splice pieces in order to help them plan their next step. "Well, now what?" Lily asked.

Chapter One Hundred Fourteen

The screen behind Emperor Hyde froze and he swung around nearly knocking the gavel off of the podium. He screamed, "How dare them? We've got to stop them. I'm calling a first, to go for an emergency bombing." He raised his gavel, "Do I have a second?" His son quickly said, "Second." He slammed the gavel down, "So be it. On the count of three, one, two,..." The President interrupted, "No you can't..." He was suddenly hit in the back of the head, knocking him to the ground. Dani felt a wave of fear come over her. She knew this meant they were both going to die and the country would be lost to the abyss.

Everyone around her held up their arms, all with an open hand. All, except two. Mr. Tobiah, who had gathered himself up, held his fist in defiance and Dani did as well. She was too young to see the Olympics, when black athletes held up their fists to symbolize black pride. She didn't really understand the full magnitude of her actions. However, at this moment, with our first black president, in defiance of tyranny, Dani felt a sense of pride swell up inside of her. *No matter what they do today I'm OK, I get it.* The gavel came crashing down, shaking the room, and the voice of evil rang out with anger and hate, "These people will bow down before death."

Chapter One Hundred Fifteen

"OK, we have five words, all Hopi in origin. They must be the clues to our fifth location."

"The five words mean what exactly?" Tiffany asked the Red Feather hologram. "Roughly, they are translated in order as; fifth, nine, ten, black and white." Tiffany and Brian looked at the words on a piece of paper. They stared at them, but thought of nothing. Wes asked, "Have you looked at the graph map thing to see where the location may be?" They pulled out the graph and the map, all six of them crowded around. Tiffany began thinking out loud, "OK, so think basic algebra. We have three numbers; nine, five and ten. What can we do with all three numbers?" Ben said, "Ninety-five, ten." Tiffany replied, "That would be way off the grid, but what about fifty-nine, ten?" Brian said, "Yeah, and look."

He drew a picture, graphing out all of the places they had been. When he connected the dots it formed a triangle. He smiled like he had really accomplished something. Tiffany hated to burst his bubble but did anyway. "That's great, but all five words are Hopi, and the main Hopi village is over in this area." She pointed back to Arizona. Wes almost choked, "-45, -50, right there." He pointed, "9 x 5 = 45, and 5 x 10 = 50, and black and white form a negative image." Then he drew a new shape in the dirt. "A star." he said, then Tiffany added, "And, it's the Hopi epicenter of Hotevilla and Oraibi." She pointed to the same spot as Wes, the Hotevilla and Oraibi area. They all looked at each other in awe. Tiffany patted Wes on the back.

Lily spoke first, "OK, we can head out, but we only have an hour left of tape before its back to live." Wes grinned, "Well, it looks like a two hour drive, so I hope you can think of something to say for an hour." Lily turned around and walked away, talking under her breath as she left, "I've been preparing for this my entire life. I'm not scared of an hour." Her confidence was contagious and the group all followed her as they walked back to the van.

Chapter One Hundred Sixteen

Another shot rang out, and another thud. *Ten in all,* Sandy thought to herself. She had no idea how close they were to her, but she knew the shots were getting closer. Her answer came quicker than she thought, when the person right next to her was questioned. "Where are they?" She couldn't place the voice. "I don't know. I'm just..." A hard slap stopped the voice of the coworker. Then, the evil voice of the man with the gun said, "We took the pleasure of getting your mother, to help give you the right motivation." Her coworker screamed, "Nooooo!" A new voice belonging to his mother pierced Sandy's ears. "I'm sorry son, I'm sorry." The young man's voice cracked as he spoke, "I don't know anything. Please don't hurt her." The gunman had no sympathy in his voice, "You have three seconds. Three, two, one..." Her coworker screamed again, "Nooooo!" The shot fired and the thud came within inches of Sandy's knees. Within seconds, she felt a warm liquid pool around her. She knew it was blood and worse she knew she was next.

Chapter One Hundred Seventeen

Tiffany and Brian lied down, back to back on the floor of the van to rest as they listened. The next forty-five minutes, was a crash course on what to say and do as they approached the Hopi village. The cube started with a dissertation on the Hopi and their beliefs, "The Hopi are a very unique tribe, and Oraibi is the oldest continuously inhabited village in North America, since around the year 1050, in your time. In 1964, the United States designated the village as a National Historic Landmark. They do not allow recording of any kind while on their land. This means the live broadcast will have to be done from the hidden camera. The city of Hotevilla has been modernized, but Oraibi still holds on to the original traditions. The Hopi are welcoming of outsiders, but they are very protective of their heritage. Red Feather and White Feather were both exiled for their radical beliefs in the prophecy. Be mindful, that this will be the first time ever that their great culture will be seen by the world."

Gavin added, "Now that the cube is a permanent uplink to the satellite, it can capture and send everything that's shot on my hidden camera. If I could get help keeping an opening in front of me, the world will have a good view." Lily added, "And we all need to speak loudly and clearly for the sound to be good." Brian questioned her, "So, what are we going to talk about?"

"That's easy, about the story of us and how we got here!" Ben interjected from the driver's seat, "The whole truth?" Lily got up, squeezed her way up next to Ben and looked directly at him, "The people deserve to know." She placed her hand on his shoulder where he was healed, "They deserve to hear it from you. The healing, it's already been seen now by the whole world. They need to feel it from your point of view." He wasn't completely convinced, but at this point, everything he had thought before this had changed. "OK. I'll do it." Lily looked at her watch and asked, "Can you go first?"

"Yeah, I guess." She looked back at Gavin, "Come up here." After a few seconds, everyone had rearranged so that Gavin could sit in the passenger seat. Now, he could get a good shot of Ben talking as he drove. Lily spoke with authority, "Quiet on the set, in five, four, three..." She poked her head into the shot and introduced Ben, "This is Officer Ben Lovato. He would like to explain the events that led up to the healing you just witnessed." She turned and disappeared from the cameras view, leaving Ben to begin, "Hi. I guess we'll start at the beginning. I got a call three days ago for a shooting at the School of Mines up in Golden."

Chapter One Hundred Eighteen

The Emperor collapsed without warning and a crew of doctors quickly removed him. As a result, the room was called to recess. Dani and President Tobiah headed back to the janitor's office that they now called home. "Mr. President?"

"Yes Dani."

"Isn't this a good thing? You look worried." He shook his head, and for the first time today, he gave a hint of stress, "I think it's not. They had already called the vote. The second in command is the former Vice President. I'm not sure if you get this vibe from him, but I'm pretty sure he's got anger issues."

"So, they're going to do it? They're going to detonate a nuke on American soil?"

"Not if I can help it."

"How can you stop it?"

"Outside of this mountain, I am still the President of the United States, and the Vice President has no idea about any of this. Many of the politicians on both sides of the spectrum are clean as well. So, we need to let them know that a plan to attack the Four Corners area has been intercepted, that should be enough to get the ball rolling. Then our military can deal with these people."

"Are you going to page them?" she said with a smirk. The President laughed, "No." He opened the door to the office and waved Dani in. As she walked in he told her, "We're going to meet them."

"How? How are we going to get out of here?" He smiled, walked over to the big shelf with cleaning supplies on it, grabbed the plunger and pulled. The entire wall and all of the shelving on it instantly swung open. Dani peered around the open wall to see a long tunnel leading down the mountain. Tobiah held out his hand, "Coming?" She stood there for a second, a little mad they hadn't left yesterday, but the feeling compelled her forward. "Wow, you're full of surprises."

As they entered the secret passageway, he closed the wall behind them. The tiny, blue lights stretched down the long cement tunnel like a runway. "What these clowns don't realize, is that unless the President is willing to play along, they have no real power. This needs to stop, and all that are involved need to be prosecuted."

"Who's going to believe us?" The President opened his finely tailored suit's jacket, revealing an IEditor, and a hidden camera on his tie, "I'm undercover." Dani giggled, "Sir, I'm not sure being you, that you can really be considered undercover."

"We have enough evidence to put these traitors away forever. Not only that, but for the first time in my lifetime, the government will actually tell the truth." The tunnel began slanting upward. "We will be able to move forward as a people. No longer will we be clinging to stale ideologies."

"Are you suggesting reworking the Constitution?"

"No, on the contrary, we will go back to the Constitution as our foundation. What we need to do, is weed out the corruption that has corroded our moral standing in the world. We must never abandon democracy and freedom."

"So what then?" The President reached a ladder that went up to a manhole. He started climbing, but continued to talk, "We start with a freeze on the Federal Reserve, and the major companies involved in today's events. Then, we call a new Continental Congress, with a wide variety of Americans, opening it to a forum on the web. This time around, we'll need to make decisions based on research and science, instead of dogma and ideology." Dani asked, while she climbed behind him, "What if the information in the artifact negates the whole government thing?" The President reached the top and grunted as he lifted the heavy, iron manhole cover up and slid it over. "We'll cross that bridge when we get there." He made it out of the opening then bent down to help Dani as she exited. "Here they come." he said as he pulled her up. She looked over to see two black Humvees with tinted windows pull up beside her. The Vice President jumped out of the first one, "Mr. President, Sir, what's the call?"

"First, make sure Dani here, stays at my side. Secondly, scramble the jets. Our guys have a two headed attack planned, and they are going to need our help with at least one front."

"What about the other one?" The President replied as he got into the Humvee, "A sleeper with a suitcase nuke has been ordered. Our only hope is for our assassin Wes, or a miracle. Has Cheyenne Mountain been shut down yet?"

The Vice President sat down, "Yes Sir. All involved are surely unaware of the prison that holds them. There is no way they could ever get past the twenty-five ton blast doors. We're also moving in on the two companies that have acted as the military arm for these traitors." The President spoke again after the Humvees had sped away, "Where are we headed?"

"We have a command center set up at the Air Force Academy."

Chapter One Hundred Nineteen

Sandy heard a loud explosion and she was shoved to the ground. She felt around, but could not find any bodies. Gun fire rang out throughout the building. She could only pray that she was being rescued. Suddenly, she was yanked up, and her mask removed. It took a second for her eyes to adjust, but in front of her, stood a soldier. "Ma'am, are you OK?"

"Yes." He reached down and grabbed his walkie-talkie, "Got another one." He pulled her across the huge empty, industrial building. The bodies on the ground were scattered among the skeletons of once great factory machines. The entire scene resembled a war zone. *Where are we?* She quickly recognized the emblem on the wall. This building was the Gates Rubber Factory, what used to be the life bread for south Denver.

She remembered visiting her grandmother at work here as a child. It was fascinating to watch the women work the assembly line, sorting belts, smoking cigarettes and gossiping at the same time. As they came close to the door she saw Captain Barba's dead body sprawled out, a large pool of blood surrounded him. Her eyes filled with tears as she stepped out into the brightness of the Denver skyline. She had to blink over and over to be able to see. When she opened her eyes, she saw a full unit of US

Marines. *Marines? On US soil?* Behind them she saw the light rail speed by.

Chapter One Hundred Twenty

As the news van pulled up, Lily finished her sentence, "The next part of the journey will be done without narration. As we are entering Hotevilla, we need to blend in." She stopped and Gavin sat facing forward, showing the camera a view of a road block. Beyond the barricades was a festival that was being held in the village center. The tribal police waved them over to a parking spot. They all exited the van. The hot summer air engulfed them as they walked towards the center of town, where a huge ceremony was taking place.

Numerous priests with dark, shoulder length hair, blunt bangs and face paint, were parading around with snakes in their mouths. As they approached, the group was terrified by what they saw, but Tiffany recognized what was taking place, "It's the Chu'tiva, the Snake-Antelope ceremony. They walk through and carry live snakes to prove their worth and their connection to nature."

As they approached, something very strange and frightening happened. All of the snakes started heading straight for them. When the snakes got near, they coiled up and went to sleep encircling the group that had just arrived. Every person at the festival stopped and looked at them. A man dressed in a Kachina costume spoke out. He was dressed like the Blue Star Kachina. He had large blue and black feather wings, traditional legging wraps, a beaded leather kilt and a pronounced golden yellow beak. Upon his head was a billowing feather headdress that covered most of his face, "What is your business here?"

Tiffany didn't hesitate she reached into the backpack and pulled out the cube. The image of both Red Feather and White Feather appeared next to one another. "Both of these men are dead, they died over twenty years ago. What is this?" Red Feather answered, "Stand brother. Pahána is here." The man was so taken aback that he took off his headdress, which is highly unorthodox in the Hopi culture, the crowd went dead silent. "Did you say Pahána?" Tiffany looked at Brian, as she thought it had to be him, but Red Feather turned and introduced Tiffany, "This is Tiffany. She has all four of the original races in her. She completes the medicine wheel. She is your Pahána. She even wears the cloak of red as your prophecy foretold." Tiffany looked down at her red Harvard sweatshirt which was now tied around her waist.

"The prophecy also says that there will be two helpers, one bearing the symbol of the sun and the other bearing the symbol of the cross. Where are they?" Brian was stunned by what the Kachina had just said, he spoke in amazement, "I have a tattoo of the sun on my arm." Wes almost choked, "I have a tattoo of a cross." Both men raised the sleeves on their left arms, revealing their symbolic markings. The man scoffed, "The reason you and your brother were exiled was crazy thoughts like this. Aah. I don't know why I'm even bothering. You're just a recording anyway..."

All of a sudden, he was interrupted by a speeding car breaking through the barricade. The silver sedan sped up as it got closer to the crowd. Suddenly, an explosion ripped the car apart. Then, something happened, the explosion instantly stopped. The car, the fire, the people standing around, everything was frozen, everything except Tiffany and the man in the feather adorned Kachina costume. "What is this? What is happening?" he asked Tiffany. She had no idea. So, she turned to the cube, "I am Pahána?"

"Yes..." The Kachina cut him off, "What about that?" He pointed at the explosion. It looked like it would have killed nearly everyone in the village. But there it was, frozen, stuck in space and time. Tiffany gazed upon it, and noticed a slight hint of some sort of electrical field surrounding the explosion. As she looked around, she noticed that everybody who was frozen had the same field. She looked at the Red Feather hologram, "Can we do anything?"

Red Feather turned and waved his fingers, the explosion started getting smaller and smaller until it was the size of a softball. He said to her, "Now, throw it towards the sun." She looked at it, then walked over and grabbed it. She couldn't possibly have believed that any of this was real, but her paradigm was rapidly shifting. She grabbed the softball size explosion and threw it like a baseball. It seemed to gain speed exponentially, until it reached the outer atmosphere and Red Feather released the energy field. It exploded high above the Earth, leaving no damage. The man in the costume was bewildered, "How did you do that? How was that possible?" Tiffany smiled and shrugged her shoulders, "You know as much as I do about that Sir."

As everyone around came to, they were confused and excited to see that the bomb was gone. Cheers rang out all around the world, as they watched people at the ceremony hugging each other and crying. What the world had just witnessed was nothing less than a miracle. The people glued to their television sets and radios worldwide were mesmerized and displayed a huge array of emotions. The man in the Kachina costume introduced himself, "I am Wikvaya, follow me. I'll take you to the key."

"So you know the key?" He looked at the cube, "I know those stones, and I'm sure Red Feather here has filled you in." Tiffany looked at Brian and then back, "No. No he didn't fill me in. In fact, he said I needed to find it on my own." He motioned for them to walk with him. The crowd parted as they made their way towards the tribal museum. Tiffany and the group followed the Kachina into the museum and straight to the back wall. There hung a single display frame with a stone in the center. The plaque below it explained that the Hopi call this the "Star Stone". Gavin had a great shot of everything. Brian reached up and pulled the frame down. He gently turned it over and opened the back, before he reached in and took out the final key. He looked up at Tiffany, "Should we put it in here?"

Red Feather and the Kachina both answered for her, "No." Red Feather's hologram spoke, "You tell them." The Kachina man explained, "It must be done at the center of Oraibi, the chosen place. You have been given a great gift young lady." Tiffany wasn't sure what gift he was referring to and had no idea what being a Pahána actually meant. She couldn't let that stand in the way. "Can we walk to Oraibi?"

"Yes, but it would be much faster if we took the school bus." They looked out into the street to see the local school bus which many of the participants in the ceremony had arrived in today. "Hurry, let's go." They walked out of the building and through the crowd, towards the yellow bus. They all entered, to find a group of elders already sitting in the back waiting.   Wikvaya started the bus, "My name means 'One Who Brings'. It is now time for me to bring you to your destiny." With that he pulled away. Everyone that was left, started running towards Oraibi, or their car, whichever was closer.

Chapter One Hundred Twenty-One

In a mobile command, control room set up specifically for this incident, the President, the head of each military branch, the Vice President and Dani all stared at the multi-screen display showing the live television feed, a map of the area and a satellite image following the approaching attack vehicles. As they reached the border of Arizona, the President gave his pilots some encouragement, "Save this country boy's." The jets streaked across the live image. When the vehicles came into focus, they were about four minutes out. A prompt at the bottom of the screen indicated this time line. The President hit a button and asked, "How far out are the jets?" Within seconds, the prompt on the screen read, "Four minutes."

Chapter One Hundred Twenty-Two

The bus pulled into the cul-de-sac that ended at the mouth of Oraibi. There were no paved streets inside the tiny village that looked like it had been warped back into time. They exited and proceeded to the center of the pueblo. In the summer heat, everyone was sweating profusely, their bodies glistening in the sun. They all sat down in a perfect circle surrounding the cube. Tiffany inserted the final key, and nothing happened, "What's wrong?" No one answered. Red Feather's hologram had disappeared when she placed the final key into the cube. She took a deep breath and instinctively put both hands on the cube.

She yanked them back when two jets came roaring up over the crest of the mesa letting their missiles fly. Gavin followed the entire episode with the hidden camera. The rocket flew about a half a mile, before the cube sprang to life and shot out several beams of blue light. The light encircled the jets, their missiles and a caravan of Firewater attack vehicles that were on their way to Oraibi. Suddenly, Red Feather's image appeared again. The missiles vanished into thin air. The blue force field that held the jets and the attack vehicles in place, slowly retracted into the cube, pulling them close to the village center. Once everyone was gathered close, he began to speak, "The

Navajo called the Hopi the Anasazi, which means 'Ancient Enemies' and many falsely know them by that name. However, the Hopi's original name was Hopituh Shi-nu-mu, which means 'The Peaceful People'. It is not in the true nature of man to harm one another. We will no longer harm each other." Instantly, the blue light flashed brightly, afterwards the jets and attack vehicles were nowhere to be seen. The crowd that was gathered around erupted in cheers.

When they turned back around, they found a strange sight. Tiffany was sitting with the cube in her lap, and her hands grasped around it. Her hair was sticking straight out, with the look of extreme static electricity. Her eyes shot out an image of on old man with a long flowing beard. He began to speak, "Hello. Do not worry about your friend's they have simply gone back to the place from which they came. I am Jodiah. I am the physical representation of the source you people call God, Jehovah or Allah. My true face looks nothing like that of yours, but to accommodate your feelings, you see this face. I was in charge of the creation that led to the human race. Because of misinformation and suppression, most of you have no idea how the world works. As a result, you have what the Hopi call Koyaaniqatis, or life out of balance. Your ignorance has broken the circle of life. Fortunately for your people, the purification period will begin on the winter solstice of 2012. If the world is in balance for the majority of the nineteen year purification, most of you will survive. If it doesn't, all of you will burn, and the fifth world will begin just like the last."

The Point of Origin

The brief pause gave Lily an opening, "Excuse me, how come we weren't warned earlier?" A checklist of dates flew up in front of the figure, he picked one out. It stated;

United Nations speech by Mr. Thomas Banyacya
December 10, 1992

"Hopi Spiritual leaders had an ancient prophecy that someday world leaders would gather in a Great House of Mica with rules and regulations to solve world problems without war. I am amazed to see the prophecy has come true and here you are today! But only a handful of United Nations Delegates are present to hear the Motee Sinom (Hopi for First People) from around the world who spoke here today.

My name is Banyacya of the Wolf, Fox and Coyote clan and I am a member of the Hopi sovereign nation. Hopi in our language means a peaceful, kind, gentle, truthful people. The traditional Hopi follows the spiritual path that was given to us by Massau'u the Great Spirit. We made a sacred covenant to follow his life plan at all times, which includes the responsibility of taking care of this land and life for his divine purpose. We have never made treaties with any foreign nation including the United States, but for many centuries we have honored this sacred agreement. Our goals are not to gain political control, monetary wealth nor military power, but rather to pray and to promote the welfare of all living beings and to preserve the world in a natural way. We still have our ancient sacred stone tablets and spiritual religious societies which are the foundations of the Hopi way of life. Our history says our White Brother should have retained those same sacred objects and spiritual foundations.

In 1948, all traditional Hopi spiritual leaders met and spoke of things I felt strongly were of great importance to all people. They selected four interpreters to carry their message of which I am the only one still living today. At that time I was given a sacred prayer feather by the spiritual leaders. I made a commitment to carry the Hopi message of peace and deliver warnings from prophecies known since the time the previous world was destroyed by flood and our ancestors came to this land.

My mission was also to open the doors of this great House of Mica to native peoples. The Elders said to knock four times and this commitment was fulfilled when I delivered a letter and the sacred prayer feather I had been given to John Washburn in the Secretary General's office in October 1991. I am bringing part of the Hopi message to you here today. We have only ten minutes to speak and time is late so I am making my statement short.

At the meeting in 1948, Hopi leaders 80, 90, and even 100 years old explained that the creator made the first world in perfect balance where humans spoke a common language, but humans turned away from moral and spiritual principles. They misused their spiritual powers for selfish purposes. They did not follow nature's rules. Eventually, their world was destroyed by sinking of land and separation of land which you would call major earthquakes. Many died and only a small handful survived.

Then this handful of peaceful people came into the second world. There they repeated their mistakes, and the world was destroyed by freezing which you call the great Ice Age.

The few survivors entered the third world. That world lasted a long time and as in previous worlds, the people spoke one language. The people invented many machines and conveniences of high technology some of which have not been seen yet in this age. They even had spiritual powers that they used for good. They gradually turned away from natural laws and pursued only material things and finally only gambling while they ridiculed spiritual principles. No one stopped them from this course and the world was destroyed by the great flood that many nations still recall in their ancient history or in their religions.

The elders said again only a small group escaped and came to this fourth world where we now live. Our world is in terrible shape again even though the Great Spirit gave us different languages and sent us to the four corners of the world and told us to take care of the Earth and all that is in it.

This Hopi ceremonial rattle represents Mother Earth. The line running around it is a time line and indicates that we are in the final days of the prophecy. What have you as individuals, as nations and as the world body been doing to take care of this Earth? In the Earth today, humans poison their own food, water and air with pollution. Many of us including children are left to starve. Many wars are still being fought. Greed and concern for material things is a common disease.

In this Western hemisphere, our homeland, many original native people are landless, homeless, starving and have no medical help. The Hopi knew humans would develop many powerful technologies that would be abused. In this century we have seen the First World War and the Second World War in which the predicted gourd of ashes which you call the atomic bomb fell from the sky with great destruction. Many thousands of people were destroyed in Hiroshima and Nagasaki.

For many years there has been great fear and danger of World War Three. The Hopi believe the Persian Gulf War was the beginning of World War Three but it was stopped and the worst weapons of destruction were not used. This is now a time to weigh the choices for our future. We do have a choice. If you, the nations of this Earth create another great war, the Hopi believe we humans will burn ourselves to death with ashes. That's why the spiritual elders stress strongly that the United Nations fully open the door for native spiritual leaders to speak as soon as possible.

Nature itself does not speak with a voice that we can easily understand. Neither can the animals and birds we are threatening with extinction talk to us. Who in this world can speak for nature and the spiritual energy that creates and flows through all life? In every continent are human beings who are like you but who have not separated themselves from the land and from nature. It is through their voice that nature can speak to us. You have heard those voices and many messages from the four corners of the world today. I have studied comparative religion and I think in your own nations and cultures you have knowledge of the consequences of living out of balance with nature and spirit. The native peoples of the world have seen and spoken to you about the destruction of their lives and homelands, the ruination of nature and the desecration of their sacred sites. It is time the United Nations used its rules to investigate these occurrences and stop them now.

The Four Corners area of the Hopi is bordered by four sacred mountains. The spiritual center within is a sacred site our prophecies say will have a special purpose in the future for mankind to survive and now should be left in its natural state. All nations must protect this spiritual center.

The Hopi and all original native people hold the land in balance by prayer, fasting, and performing ceremonies. Our spiritual elders still hold the land in the Western Hemisphere in balance for all living beings including humans. No one should be relocated from their sacred homelands in this Western Hemisphere or anywhere in the world. Acts of forced relocation such as Public Law 93531 in the United States must be repealed.

The United Nations stands on our native homeland. The United Nations talks about human rights, equality and justice and yet the native people have never had a real opportunity to speak to this assembly since its establishment until today. It should be the mission of your nations and this assembly to use your power and rules to examine and work to cure the damage people have done to this Earth and to each other. Hopi elders know that was your mission and they wait to see whether you will act on it now.

Nature, the First People and the spirit of our ancestors are giving you loud warnings. Today, December 10, 1992, you see increasing floods, more damaging *hurricanes, hail storms, climate changes and earthquakes as our prophecies said would come. Even animals and birds are warning us with strange change in their behavior such as the beaching of whales. Why do animals act like they know about Earth's problems and most humans act like they know nothing? If we humans do not wake up to the warnings, the great purification will come to destroy this world just as the previous worlds were destroyed.*

(Thomas and Oren Lyons held up a picture of a large rock drawing in Hopiland.)

This rock drawing shows part of the Hopi prophecy. There are two paths. The first with high technology but separate from natural and spiritual law leads to these jagged lines representing chaos. The lower path is one that remains in harmony with natural law. Here we see a line that represents a choice like a bridge joining the paths. If we return to spiritual harmony and live from our hearts we can experience a paradise in this world. If we continue only on this upper path, we will come to destruction.

It's up to all of us, as children of Mother Earth to clean up this mess before it's too late. The elders request that during this International Year for the World's Indigenous Peoples, the United Nations keep that door open for spiritual leaders from the four comers of the world to come to speak to you for more than a few minutes as soon as possible. The elders also request that eight investigative teams visit the native areas of the world, observe and tell the truth about what is being done and stop these nations from moving in this self destructive direction.

If any of you leaders want to learn more about the spiritual vision and power of the elders, I invite you to come out to Hopiland and sit down with our real spiritual leaders in their sacred Kivas where they will reveal the ancient secrets of survival and balance.

I hope that all members of this assembly that know the spiritual way will not just talk about it but in order to have real peace and harmony, will really follow what it says across the United Nations wall: 'They shall beat their swords into plowshares and study war no more.' Let's together do that now!"[1]

The speech lasted two minutes, and no one could believe what they had seen or heard. Red Feather's image looked right at Gavin's camera, "That speech was delivered on December 10, 1992, any other questions?" Tiffany quickly asked, "The old man said I was a trigger. What does that mean?"

"Pahána, to the Hopi, the true White Brother is you." When you touched this rock, you were given a very special gift. This gift could help save your people, but they need to change. You ask what you are the trigger to. The knowledge you now posses is the trigger, the trigger to the future, to the starting gun for the fifth world. The trigger started when you were born. For the rest of you, I understand that belief is in short supply. So, for your viewing pleasure, I give you..."

He clapped his hands and a bright white light shot out of his eyes, piercing everyone's sight who was watching. Then he said, "Anyone who just saw this, you have just been given the gift of perfect sight." People in the crowd took off their glasses. Screams and cries started to disseminate throughout the crowd. People were overcome with joy. The figure smiled, evidently pleased with himself, "I will communicate with the Pahána from now on. Until then, it's up to you." He pointed out to the people of the world.

The figure shrank back into the cube. Lily wasn't sure if they were still live. She went ahead anyway, and it was a good thing she did because the cube continued to broadcast just like it had said it would. Lily walked over to Tiffany, "So, where do we go from here?" Tiffany looked at Brian, who grabbed her hand tightly, "Obviously the world has some decisions to make, and we'll be there for them, but right now we need some sleep."

In the background, thousands of paratroopers were landing, coming in to protect the crew and the device. Lily got the hint from Brian, who was standing in silence. For the first time in his life he felt that silence was a blessing and not a curse. He remained standing silently, taking in the historical event they had just been part of. She turned to Wes and Ben, "Any comments?" Ben looked at the hidden camera and got down on one knee, "Will you marry me Sandy?"

***

Sandy was in a prep tent that the Marines had set up outside of the Gates Rubber Factory, watching the whole event unfold. She jumped up and down screaming. "Yes! Yes! Yes!"

The Point of Origin

***

Tears streamed down the face of Gavin, who couldn't contain his emotions. Wes leaned in. "I'm retiring for good this time."

***

Dani and the President shared a huge hug. "Dani, I would like to offer you a spot in my administration. I hope you will consider it." Dani's tears couldn't be stopped, but behind the sobbing, she was resolute, "Sir, it would be my pleasure." He turned to walk out of the trailer, "You coming? We've got to get back to Washington. There's a lot of work to be done. Change is happening now."

References

[1]Banyacya, Thomas. "The Hopi Message to the United
     Nations General Assembly." *Hopi Traditional Elder
     Thomas Banyacya's Message to the World.* Smoke Signals,
     1992. Web. 2 June 2010.
     http://banyacya.indigenousnative.org/banyacya.html.

About the Authors

Duke and Nancy Kell are educators and authors. This Yin and Yang duo are partners in every aspect of life. Residing on the Big Island of Hawai'i, with their two daughters, their passion for knowledge drives their constant creativity.